PRAISE FOR SUE DENVER'S WEREWOLF FOR HIRE

"By the end of it I didn't know if I wante
or cry because I already want the next
great binge read!"

— *THE INTERNATIONAL REVIEW OF BOOKS*

"If you like the idea of a badass female main character getting the upper hand and beating a few powerful, rich bad guys, pick up *Werewolf for Hire*."

— *SCRIBBLE'S WORTH BOOK REVIEWS*

"A thought-provoking mystery that goes one step beyond the usual whodunit (or, who will do it) scenario."

— *MIDWEST BOOK REVIEW*

WEREWOLF FOR HIRE

SUE DENVER

JGF PRESS

Werewolf for Hire by Sue Denver, at SueDenver.com and WolfLady.net

Published by JGF Press, at JGFpress.com

Published February 7, 2023 by JGF Press, Crossville TN

SARA FLORES' WORLD

- Sara's world is our everyday, normal world.
- Nobody believes in werewolves, vampires or anything supernatural.
- Sara was turned into a werewolf by her former neighbor Joe White Wolf — right before he died.
- Sara thinks she's the only werewolf on earth, but she hopes (or fears) she's wrong.
- Lupiti elders remember their grandfathers talk about seeing old Joe White Wolf turn into a wolf during tribal ceremonies — way back in the late 1800's.
- This tells Sara she may have a very, very long life — if her new lifestyle doesn't get her killed.

1

Werewolf for Hire
By Sue Denver

Lillian Knudsen shook yet another hand and gave yet another distracted smile. The Tulsa Chamber of Commerce rubber chicken lunch sat uneasily in her stomach — a burp just made her re-taste it. She patted her red hair to make sure it wasn't falling out of the biz-exec bun she always wore to events like this — so much fussier than normal.

She'd chatted up the Caskcuts, who were at her table for the lunch. They'd bought the downtown hardware store and were hoping to learn more about how business operates in Tulsa, Oklahoma.

She'd made the rounds of hellos to everyone else.

All she really wanted to do was get to her Jeep, go home and pass out. Except... she was afraid to sleep. Afraid the dreams would come again. Like they had for the past two weeks.

Fourteen years ago, a bomb blew up the truck she was driving in Iraq and took her left foot. She'd had nightmares about it for five years — waking up in soaking wet sheets with her heart racing.

Bo Knudsen had been there for Lillian — in the hospital, then in marriage, and finally as her partner in their shooting range business.

When cancer took him two years ago, she didn't know how she managed — only that the demands of the business kept her out of the hole she wanted to crawl into.

Love for Bo — and the life they built — had made the nightmares go away so long ago she'd stopped thinking about them.

Two weeks ago, they came back. Which is why she was craving sleep at 1:30 in the afternoon.

A hand grabbed her shoulder. Lillian flinched.

"My goodness," said Betty Sue Franken, her helmet hair gorgeously styled as always and probably hard as a rock. "I didn't mean to scare you."

Lillian winced.

"I just wanted to say it's always good to see you. We women business owners have to stick together, you know." Betty Sue actually winked at her, then patted her on the shoulder. She turned to greet someone else before Lillian could even respond. Just as well.

Lillian spotted Warren Caddel, owner of Sharp Shooters gun shop, across the room. She turned away. The annoying man was trying to buy up half of Tulsa.

She shouldn't have come today. She usually liked these events. It was fun playing business leader in town — not a role she'd ever imagined for herself. She'd always thought she'd be a nurse — until Desert Storm hospitals changed her mind.

Lillian had adjusted her left leg prosthesis today to allow her to wear low heels with her best business suit. But she'd been in a rush and, apparently, she hadn't adjusted it perfectly — her left leg was tilted for a slightly higher heel than the one her shoe had.

It was frustrating how the tiniest difference could make walking feel unnatural.

She waved goodbye to the others, then took the garage elevator up a floor. She walked towards her bright red Jeep Wrangler hardtop, parked about 20 cars away.

She winced as she saw the two-week-old mashed-in front hood she had yet to get repaired. It looked like someone had swung a baseball bat down on it, but why? It made no sense.

A car engine revved behind her, so she moved over closer to the cars on her left to give the driver more room to get by.

Something hit her good right leg, crumpling it. Her body flew forward, slamming into a blue Chevy, bashing her head on the trunk.

She slid, dazed, to the dirty concrete floor.

What the heck?

Who?

Lillian looked around. She was on the floor, her head leaning against the back of the Chevy.

Tires squealed so she stuck her head out and looked. A red taillight turned the far corner, speeding towards the exit.

Gone.

Lillian saw blood on her knees, her nylons scraped to shreds. She stared blankly at them.

Suddenly, her stomach dropped. She was flying through the air from bombs, hearing the staccato of rifles shooting, the M14s returning fire. There were screams. Terrible screams. The stench of smoke was everywhere. Her silk blouse was wringing wet, and her heart was having hysterics.

She covered her head and ears with her hands and arms and pulled her head down to her knees.

"Not there. Not there. I'm not there." She said it over and over like the V.A. therapist had suggested to her.

She didn't know how long she stayed, sitting on the dirty concrete floor, arms over her head.

The next thing she noticed was the chime of the garage elevator. Someone was getting out. She shook her head and tried to stand. Her right leg hurt, but it could hold her. Her prosthesis wasn't damaged.

Lillian brushed off her legs and skirt and walked the rest of the way to her Jeep. She flashed the Jeep remote, entered and buckled up. She sat there, taking deep breaths, trying to slow her heart rate.

A gun! She needed a gun to protect herself!

Only then did she feel the Springfield Armory 911 she had holstered at her back. Sitting there. Still holstered.

Angry at herself, she leaned forward and pulled it out. She stared at it and shook her head. What was the point of going armed if you forgot it was there when you needed it? Bo would have been disappointed in her. *She* was disappointed in her.

She laid it on the seat beside her. After more deep breaths, she checked the rearview mirror and backup camera carefully.

Lillian looked everywhere when she exited the garage, but no cars sat idling — waiting for her. She was on edge the entire drive home. Cars moving towards her caused her hands to clench — she expected them to swerve into her. She was afraid of cars coming up from behind her. She flinched when cars passed her, expecting them to jerk the wheel into her.

She almost cried in relief when she finally spotted her comforting red brick house with its wide swath of green lawn and green foundation plantings. The green always soothed her, reminded her that although the temperatures could boil past 100 here in Tulsa, she was not — absolutely not — still in that hellhole Iraqi desert.

The remote opened the garage door and welcomed her back into the womb. Sanctuary. The place Bo bought for them. One story, so she never had to deal with stairs. A pool in the back, which he was so proud of. But which she hadn't used in the two years since he died.

Lillian got out of the car and found herself staring — again — at the dent on her front hood. Her peace evaporated. Nausea started to rise in her throat.

Turning purposefully away from it, she used her gun to enter her own house as though it were enemy territory. She went through it carefully, checking all doors and windows. Checking under beds and in closets. Resetting the house alarm for the night.

Satisfied she was safe — for now — she sat down on Bo's big recliner. Paws, the black alleycat with white feet Bo had adopted, jumped up in her lap and started to purr. She petted the cat, and finally, finally, her heart rate slowed back down.

She slept like a rock that night. She wasn't sure if it was physical or mental exhaustion, but a full night of sleep did wonders. She went to work feeling positive for a change.

Maybe she'd turned the corner?

But... Lillian jumped at noises. She patted her gun behind her back obsessively. She felt like her 22-year-old self again — afraid of everything. Vulnerable.

She hadn't turned any corner.

By 4:30 that afternoon, Lillian gave up. Her problem wasn't going away. Somebody had — probably — hit her car with a baseball bat. Yesterday, someone had slammed their car into her. She needed a professional to find out what the heck was going on here. And to fix it.

2

Sara Flores liked BK's Shooting Range. If you needed to carry a firearm, and Sara did, then you needed to practice. She had tried other local indoor ranges but came away covered in black lead soot — which meant she was also inhaling it. She really didn't want or need anything that could make her stupider than she sometimes already was.

At BK's range, you only shoot BK's ammunition which had lead-free primer plus copper bullets. Clean air.

Sara liked their pistol booth four — which was mostly hidden from the other booths. Hidden was important because Sara's reflexes were better than human. Noticeably better.

It wasn't any fun coming in twice a week just to hit the bullseye with all 60 rounds. Her vision was normal, but her muscles held her hand unnaturally steady.

Others might be satisfied shooting this well, but Sara wasn't. She worried she needed to be better.

It was a year and a half since she was turned werewolf by a Lupiti shaman who then died on her. In that time Sara mounted seven rescue missions — each to help some innocent targeted by someone evil who thought he could use them or kill them without consequences.

She'd succeeded in each of those missions — but luck played a bigger factor than she was comfortable with. Sara still worried she wasn't good enough. She had no special forces training. No martial arts.

She'd recently earned her Private Investigator license for Oklahoma, but what did that really mean? It required only 55 hours of training and passing a test. Voila! — she was now a P.I. She felt like she'd "earned" one of those mail-order diplomas sold on the Internet.

So Sara came to BK's twice a week — trying to get better. She liked to practice drawing a pistol from her different concealed carry holsters. From the front and then the back, right hand then left. That was 40 shots. Then she used her corset holster, which fit right up under her breasts. Ten shots with the right hand, then 10 with the left. As fast as she could.

Sara hit the button to bring the target back to her.

She wasn't perfect today. For a change, she'd tried shooting from a different start. She had turned past 90 degrees from the target — as far as she could while still clearly seeing it from her peripheral vision. Most of her shots were no longer dead center, and two had just missed the bulls eye. Something to work on the next time she was here.

Sara packed up and left the booth.

She was walking past the front desk when Lillian Knudsen, the owner, called her name. Lillian was a conservative woman with long red hair tied back at her nape in the kind of ponytail women wore when they were no longer in their 20s. Not high up like a real pony's.

Word was Lillian and her husband started this range when they returned together from serving in Iraq. For the past two years, Lillian ran it herself. Sara liked her quiet confidence in dealing with the occasional gun nut who demanded to use his own ammo.

Lillian held out a folded paper towards Sara. "You left this on the desk when you paid," she said, looking intently — strangely — at Sara.

"Oh," Sara said. She walked to the counter and took the paper. It looked like one of the payment receipts given out at BK's Range. "Thanks."

Lillian immediately looked down as though she were working. Sara took the hint and walked out the door, putting the paper in her purse.

She didn't want to drive all the way home before reading it, so she pulled her Ford F-150 over at the bright red "Cane's" sign and got into the drive-through for Raising Cane's Chicken Fingers. She got her usual Three Finger Combo with unsweetened tea for an early dinner. She backed into a parking spot where she could see everyone and dug in. In between bites, she opened the paper from Lillian.

It read: "I heard you're a new P.I. Call me at this number and tell me where to meet safely away from here. Now, if possible. Urgent."

Sara's eyebrows raised. This was unexpected.

She got her P.I. license mainly to give cops an explanation in case they found her near dead bodies, as had happened in the past. Bodies she had caused to be dead. She never planned to make it a business. Her name wasn't on her office door, and she had no phone listing.

But this note was a plea for help. From someone Sara liked and admired. She couldn't ignore it and leave the woman hanging. She at least needed to figure out what it was about.

Sara finished dinner, licked the "special sauce" off of her fingers, and stuffed the remains in the bag.

She pulled out her phone and looked up BK's Range. The listing said they closed at 6 PM. Her watch said it was now 5:30.

The phone listed on the note was different from the main listing. Was it Lillian's personal phone? Was she worried her work phone was tapped? But if that were true, wouldn't her cell be tapped too?

How should she...?

Sara nodded at the idea. A personal cell is used for friends.

She called.

Lillian answered, "Yes?"

"Girlfriend, I got cause to *celebrate* today!" said Sara, voice excited. "Can you get away for dinner? I'm buying!"

There was a pause on the line. Then Lillian said, "Sure. When and where?"

"I'm thinking that great Home Cookin' restaurant on West 4th Street. What time can you make it?"

"I could be there about 6:30."
"Sounds great! You won't believe my news! See you!"
Sara hung up.

3

Sara had picked her office location carefully. It was downtown, where there were lots of people at different times. It was in a building which also housed a dry cleaner, an attorney and an audiologist doctor group. Anyone might have a good reason to go into the building.

Another benefit — the back entry to the building faced the back entry of Home Cookin' restaurant. A person could eat there and slip out into the back alley and go right into the back of her building.

She kept a small rack of clothes, wigs and shoes there — changes of identity, actually. Because she didn't plan to take clients, she'd thrown in a beat up Salvation Army desk and three chairs. In case she needed to hang out there for a few hours.

It had its own bathroom.

Because Lillian was coming, she wanted to sweep the place for bugs. Sara delegated all tech stuff to her tech guru, Mason Spencer. Unfortunately, the man lived in Pennsylvania — which meant he gave her the tools, but she had to do the physical work.

Following Mason's instructions, she did a visual scan with her eyeballs, followed by a radio frequency scan with a device that also picks up microwave transmissions. Plus another scan for infrared and visible light emitters.

It was so ridiculously much, Sara decided she would beg Mason to fly in and install security in the office comparable to her home. Then nobody could get in to plant all these hypothetical bugs. And — if they somehow did get in — she could see who they were and what they did.

Sara finished the scans without finding anything. She checked her watch. It was time to head to the restaurant.

She looked in the bathroom mirror and grinned. Not too bad. She was mid-30s, 5' 6" and thanks to her new super-metabolism could eat anything without gaining weight. She checked her blond wig to make sure it was straight. She was grateful her brown shag hairstyle was pretty short — it made wearing a wig tolerable. Wigs would never fit on her head if she had a bunch of hair to cram up under the things.

Sara took the stairs down instead of the elevator. She opened the back door to the building and looked. Occasionally she would see a delivery van in the alley — or someone taking out trash to the bins behind the restaurant. Right now, all was clear.

Home Cookin' was great for her purposes because there were tables in different nooks — behind half walls and plants. You couldn't stand at the door — or even in the middle of the restaurant — and see everyone eating there.

Lillian was on one of the chairs near the door for people waiting to be seated. Sara greeted her with a hug, then put an arm around her and led her back into the restaurant, saying, "I've got a table in the back."

Sara caught the eye of the manager, held up two fingers, and nodded. The man nodded back. He would charge $100 ($50 each) to the credit card number she had given him.

"Let's freshen up first," she said and steered Lillian and herself into a solo restroom. She locked the door and put a finger to her lips.

Sara handed Lillian a card. On it, she had written, "Pull out any electronics you're carrying, including cell phone, USB drive, car starter, and all credit cards." Sara pulled out a Faraday bag and opened it. Lillian removed everything and put it into the bag. Sara closed it and handed it back to Lillian.

Sara then pulled out a scanner and ran it over Lillian's body. Carefully. With special attention on her jacket and her shoes. The light stayed green.

Sara turned the card over. It said, "Come with me, but stay silent." Lillian nodded. Sara took them out the back of the restaurant, across the alley, and into the back door of her office building.

Once inside her office, Sara locked the door and took back the Faraday bag. She put it in the small bathroom, turned on the white noise machine she had sitting on top of the toilet, then closed the door. She pulled two chairs so they faced each other — as far from the bathroom as the small room allowed. She sat down and smiled.

"Sorry to go so 'James Bond' on you," Sara said, "but I figured if someone as capable as you needed help, it must be serious."

Lillian took a deep breath and settled more into the chair. She looked around at the plain, mostly empty box. Then at Sara.

"I've tried to tell myself," Lillian said, "it's all coincidence. But... if it looks like a duck and quacks like a duck..."

Lillian told Sara what happened in the parking garage the day before. "I got a bruise the size of Texas on my right thigh. But I'd be dead if that was what this guy wanted. He could have plowed right into me instead of knocking me down."

Sara waited for more, but Lillian was quiet.

"Forgive me for being blunt," Sara said, "but your skin and your eyes — they look like you've barely slept in a week. What aren't you telling me?"

Lillian nodded. "Two weeks. I haven't slept in two weeks. That's when someone took a baseball bat to the hood of my jeep. It was annoying, but I dismissed it."

"Nobody heard anything?"

"No. The range is soundproof, as you know. The parking lot is pretty isolated — there's usually nobody around when I close up."

Lillian rubbed her hands over her face.

"And?" asked Sara.

"Last week, I got in the Jeep after work and I smelled gas. I called my mechanic — he shoots at my range — and he came to look at it. He towed it to his shop. He said the gas tank was cracked. He said it looked like a sharp rock had punctured it."

Sara's eyes went wide. "Driving it could have killed you, right? If there was a spark and the tank exploded?"

"Yeah, except... the gas stench was really strong. Tim noticed it immediately. Said it was much stronger than he'd expect. And I'm really sensitive to gasoline. From Iraq."

"Nothing on your parking lot camera?" Sara asked.

Lillian shook her head. "Someone turned the camera away when my jeep got dented. So I added a fixed camera with a bracket that holds it still. But it got spray-painted black on the lens before the gas incident. Now I have one so high you'd have to bring a ladder to spray it."

Sara got up. She had a small mini fridge in the office — with no "smart" electronics in it. "I got Diet Coke and water," she offered.

Lillian nodded at the water. "Smart lady," said Sara, handing her a water and grabbing a Diet Coke for herself.

Sara sat back down and took a drink. She liked how the drink burned its way down the throat. It was a very stupid thing to like, but she did.

"So," Sara said, "who would want to scare you and/or hurt you?"

"That's the biggest problem. I've spent hours thinking about it, and I can't imagine anyone who would do this. And before you ask, I'm not dating right now. I'm not suing anyone."

"What about guys you banned from the range?"

"Yeah, some of them got hot, but they got over it. This is Oklahoma. There are tons of ranges they can go to besides mine."

"Enemies of your late husband?"

Lillian shook her head. "He's been dead two years. I really doubt it."

"Could it be one of your regular customers?"

Lillian shook her head. "I sure hope not. But... but whoever it is seems familiar with the range."

"Could money be a motive?"

"I don't think so. I do own the business outright. But I have no relatives, and I've told a number of people I'm leaving everything to the Wounded Warriors Project."

Sara considered. "It could be escalating towards murder. But it sounds more like they want you frightened — badly frightened. Is there some guy hanging around trying hard to be a friend? Who might want you scared enough to start depending on him? Maybe it's a long game to get you dependent on him and then get you and your business?

Lillian sighed. "Darn it. I don't want to suspect everyone. There's a few guys I banter with. Flirt with a little. But it doesn't mean anything."

She thought some more. "At least it doesn't mean anything to me."

4

"Okay," said Sara. "I'll watch the parking lot tomorrow. But I believe with your high camera they'll go after you elsewhere. I'm most worried about you at home — because that would be the next location in their progression. Here's what we should do." And Sara told her.

They retraced their steps back to the restaurant then walked out the front together. They strolled, laughing, to Lillian's Jeep. Sara watched her get in and waved as she drove away.

Sara walked a few blocks to the Oklahoma University hospital and went in the main doors. She loved the place because it had several exits from different parts of the building. She left through a door to the coffee shop — far from the main door — and made her way to her covered parking garage. Then she drove to an all-night convenience store about ten blocks from Lillian's house.

Lillian was waiting. Sara got into the back seat of Lillian's Jeep and under a blanket there. Lillian drove home and, using her electronic garage door opener, drove directly into the garage and closed the door. Sara had her Rugar LC9 out, but nobody was waiting for them.

Except Paws, the black cat. Paws took one look at Sara — one sniff of her — and ran away to hide. The rest of the night, whenever Sara would feel eyes on her, she'd find Paws. Hiding behind a sofa or a door. Staring at her.

The house was homey. Ranch-style western with rough wood floors — but fancied up because they were laid in a chevron pattern. It had a sense of humor — three primary-colored pictures of cows sat over the fireplace. The furniture was upscale good-ole-boy comfortable.

Sara was most impressed with Lillian's house alarm system. It had outside infrared cameras, and every window, door and outside vent was wired.

"Bo did it," Lillian said. "He was afraid someone might think we keep guns here. Because of the range."

Sara was also impressed — stunned even — at the number of guns Lillian kept in the house. There were two shotguns — one under the bed and one in the hall closet. She had three handguns in addition to the one she wore everywhere. One was kept in a bedside table, another in the office desk drawer and the last one in a kitchen drawer. When Sara recommended she add an ankle holster gun, for the time being, Lillian turned up yet another gun she had in the house — a subcompact Sig P365.

Sara raised her eyebrows at Lillian.

Lillian crossed her arms over her chest. "You try sleeping alone with one leg and see how many guns *you* want around the house."

Sara suddenly focused on the gun Lillian wore at her back. The one she apparently wore everywhere. "You had it on yesterday?" she asked.

Lillian looked down at her feet. "The car was gone by the time I was able to look for it."

"Okaaay."

Sara looked at Lillian. "What did you do in Iraq?"

"Support personnel. I mainly drove a truck."

Sara didn't say anything.

"I'm qualified with guns. I just..."

Sara held up her hands. "I'm sure you're qualified." She continued her search of the house. She was relieved to find no planted cameras or microphones.

Lillian moved into the kitchen and opened the fridge. Sara was astonished at all the food inside. Healthy food too, including multiple types of leafy green things. Lillian pulled out lettuce, avocados, turkey and some kind of sprouts, and soon Sara was eating the best sandwich she'd had in a long time.

Sara asked Lillian about Iraq and spent the next two hours listening — and laughing — at Lillian's descriptions of military snafus and young, dumb soldiers. Occasionally Lillian fidgeted or ran her fingers threw her hair — and Sara realized she was editing out the very bad parts.

About 10 PM, Lillian retired to her bedroom and went to sleep. Sara eventually fell asleep on the brown suede sofa, staring up at the pictures on the wall, especially one cow's soulful turquoise eyes.

...Only to be awakened by a scream from the bedroom.

Oh, no! she leapt to her feet, grabbed her gun, and ran to Lillian's room. *How could someone get in?*

Sara threw open the door, rushed in, then put on the brakes.

Nobody but Lillian was in the room. Lillian was lying on the four-poster bed, curled on her side into as tight a ball as she could. The white bedspread and sheets were kicked off. Her body shone with sweat. Her hands were holding the pillow over her head, and she was breathing in fast gasps.

Sara started to move to the bed. To comfort.

Lillian was saying, over and over, almost in a whisper — "I'm not there. Not there. I'm really not there."

Realizing there was no imminent danger and feeling like an intruder, Sara backed out of the room. She was very sure Lillian would not want anyone to see her like this. She eased the door closed and went back to her couch.

In the morning, they made plans for the day. Sara was relieved Lillian had someone else who opened the gun range for her — so Lillian wouldn't be there alone.

"I can't hang out inside with you without blowing my cover, but I'll be nearby — you can call or text. I'll follow you to the range, but have your gun out and ready while you drive and walk into your range. And keep it easy to access all day. Don't snap your holster closed.

"Call me if you need to go anywhere. Otherwise, I'll be watching before you close and follow you home."

5

It was 6:30 PM when Lillian finished tallying the day's receipts and locking the cash and checks in the safe for deposit the next day. She stepped outside and locked the outer door.

Her heart sped up. She looked carefully at the small parking lot, lit by one mediocre streetlight. Her Jeep was the only vehicle remaining, as usual. Darn it, she hated this fear. She pulled out her cell phone and speed dialed Sara.

"Everything alright?" Lillian asked.

"Looks good so far," Sara responded. "I checked your car for explosives two hours ago. And nobody has been by it since."

"Where are you?"

"You're facing me. I'm half a block away, parked among the U-Haul trucks. Facing you."

Lillian looked up. "Good job. I can't spot you."

Holding her gun at the side of her leg, Lillian walked quickly to the Jeep, got in, and locked the doors. She put her gun on the seat beside her and buckled up. She stuck her cell phone in the cradle and plugged it into the USB port. She breathed a sigh of relief as she drove out of the lot and onto the street. Soon she was on the I-44.

Lillian shook her head. She couldn't imagine someone trying to hurt her. Why? Maybe the car hitting her was an accident? Someone distracted by a cell phone? Someone who raced out of the garage to avoid the consequences? She couldn't have Sara living at her house forever.

Lillian yawned. The nightmares came again last night. She badly needed real sleep. Uninterrupted sleep.

Ten minutes later, Lillian slowed down as the interchange came up. She flicked on her right turn signal to switch lanes.

Something strange caught her attention from the corner of her left eye, and she turned her head toward it. Out her driver's side window she saw a beat-up gray pickup truck two lanes over.

Its headlights had turned and were now pointed right at her Jeep. Nobody was in the lanes between them so there was nothing in its path.

In shock, she raised her eyes and saw the driver. He was a young man with short brown hair and the most determined look on his face. He was staring right at her Jeep — not at her but at the Jeep. His eyes were glaring, with a look of total satisfaction growing his face. Like he was seconds away from winning a Grand Slam. Like he was about to claim a million dollars. The top prize.

She watched as he closed the distance between them. Very fast.

Lillian stomped hard on her gas pedal to get past him. But seconds later, there was a loud bang as the truck plowed into her driver's side door. It was a double punch. First the truck hit the side of her Jeep, and then the front seat bags exploded into what must have been large, sharp-edged rocks.

They *hurt*!

Her car skidded sideways while still speeding forward.

The truck pushed her into the right lane. Thankfully nobody was across from her.

Lillian turned. The edge of the overpass was rushing towards her. If she went off the edge... down into traffic...

She screamed.

Her jeep was shoved onto the shoulder, and still it kept moving. The overpass was ending — the cloverleaf turnoff was coming up.

Lillian used all the strength of her good right leg to get a little more speed from the gas pedal.

She jerked her car wheel towards the truck — trying to stay away from the edge of the overpass. But it didn't make any difference.

There was another loud bang, and her head slammed back against the seat as her jeep jerked forward — faster than before. The airbags deflated. They looked like limp flags of surrender.

Lillian's Jeep hit the guardrail, slamming her hard against the seatbelt. Her hands flew off the wheel. She had only a second to pray, but it wasn't answered. Her Jeep tipped up on the right wheels.

Lillian tilted onto her right side, then continued the spin. She was upside down and falling. Tumbling.

Lillian closed her eyes.

6

Sara had been driving about 200 feet behind Lillian, talking on her phone to Mason, her Pennsylvania tech guy who was also her friend.

She'd rescued Mason about a year ago from oil company goons planning to kill him for what he found hacking their system. In the gunfight to save him, she'd been forced to transform into wolf in front of Mason. Instead of being horrified, Mason told her it was "lit," and he wanted to be a part of it.

Sara had made him wait until he graduated — hoping he'd change his mind. But Mason never wavered and joined her small crusade right after graduating. And Sara was very grateful, despite her worries about endangering him.

"I'm not finding anything on her husband that points to a grudge," Mason said. "Nobody filed anything on him. He didn't accuse anyone of anything. If he got into a fight with anybody — or if she did — it wasn't written up."

"Thanks," said Sara, sighing. Motive was proving elusive on this case.

Sara looked up. A truck up ahead smashed into the side of Lillian's Jeep.

"Shit!" She hit the accelerator, closing the distance.

"What can I do?" she asked herself aloud.

She couldn't get to the right of the truck to push it back.

She couldn't see the driver.

The biggest danger was Lillian could be pushed off the overpass into traffic.

Sara raced her F-150 up onto the right shoulder and slammed it into the back of Lillian's Jeep — pushing it forward as hard as her truck could. Trying to move it forward past the drop-off.

There was a gut-wrenching screech of metal, and the right guardrail gave as the Jeep hit it, teetered, then toppled, falling over the railing and tumbling like clothes in a dryer.

But — thank god! — the Jeep had made it past the drop-off and was rolling down the hillside of the cloverleaf.

Sara gasped in air. She must have been holding her breath.

The Jeep's tumbling slowed as the ground flattened. Its roof hit a guardrail at the bottom of the circle, and the underside rose, trying to flip again. It didn't make it. The wheels thudded back to the ground.

The beater pickup that had attacked the Jeep turned back onto the highway and sped away.

Sara read the license plate out loud. Hopefully, Mason was still on the line, although she couldn't see her phone. It must be on the floor somewhere.

She wanted to go after the guy. Badly.

But she had to help Lillian.

Sara took the off ramp, drove around the circle, and pulled up tight against the guardrail. She grabbed her first aid kit and ran to the Jeep. She could only see the hardtop, and the sight wasn't encouraging. It was cracked almost in half, and one part was shoved far inside. She couldn't see Lillian. There was a lot of glass.

She got to what was left of the front windshield and finally saw Lillian. Strapped in. At first glance, she looked okay — the roll-bar had held up.

Sara remembered the "ABC" acronym. Airways? They were fine. Breathing? Yes, she was. Circulation? Lillian had a pulse. Sara looked for anything that might indicate bleeding and saw nothing. Her left leg — the one with the prosthesis was bent a little funny. Better not to move her.

Sara sat down on the grass. She hit the phone icon on her iWatch and called 911. She told them she needed an ambulance.

Sara tried to slow her heartbeat. She wanted to beat the crap out of something, she was so angry. At herself. At not knowing what to do. In her worst nightmares, Sara dreamed her lack of training would get a client killed. It almost did tonight.

Instead of bemoaning that she had no special forces training, she should damn well hire someone to teach her. And... she obviously needed an intensive driving course for bodyguards.

She would get them both. Just as soon as she stopped whoever wanted to kill Lillian. Stopped them permanently.

7

Clyde Ruskin pounded his gloved hand on the steering wheel of the stolen beater pickup truck and yelled, "Yes!" at the top of his lungs. His uncle would have to be impressed with this. Not only did he knock her over the railing, but he also got away clean!

So who's the fuckup now? Not him, for damn sure!

He couldn't wait to dump the stolen truck and have it out with Uncle Warren. His ears still burned from the the way the man had talked to him this morning. Accusing him of lying about the bitch. Saying he probably didn't hit her in the parking lot.

Damnit, he hit her perfectly. Exactly like Warren wanted. Enough to knock her down but not kill her.

He was tired of this shit. The man was always putting him down. It was time he got some respect. Time Uncle Warren treated him more like a partner instead of some hired hand.

For a moment, he remembered the truck that had come out of nowhere and hit the Jeep. Right before it went over. But it was nothing. It was a positive even. He still got the job done. Mission accomplished. He noticed his fingers were drumming on the wheel and forced them to stop. He was going to demand some respect.

Clyde pulled into the huge parking lot behind Hooters. He

smoothed down his black hair in the mirror and gave himself a wink, then left the keys on the seat in clear view with the doors unlocked.

He looked around and saw Uncle Warren's Lincoln pull in about 10 cars away. He walked over and got in the soft leather passenger seat. Warren drove out of the lot and back onto the freeway.

Clyde hadn't expected much praise — it wasn't Uncle Warren's way. But damnit, would a "Good job" kill the man to say? And why wasn't he saying anything at all? Finally, he couldn't stand the silence.

"Well?" he asked.

He looked over at Uncle Warren. The man just sat there, driving down the road, looking important with his hundred dollar hair cut and his graying temples. And what the hell was with that? The guy wasn't even 40. He probably had them dyed to make him look "distinguished" instead of like the good-ole-boy roots they both came from.

"Well?" he asked again. Acid ate his stomach. His fingers were tapping his knee again.

Finally, Warren glanced at him, then back at the road. His voice came out soft. "She was supposed to land on the freeway below."

"Yeah, well, that other truck screwed that. You shouldn't've had two of us doing the same thing. Be glad I got the job done."

"I didn't hire the second truck."

"Huh? Whatdaya mean? It hit her too."

"I did not hire anyone else."

"Then who was it?"

"I'll find out soon. I got the license plate."

Warren looked at him again. "As for you — you'd better hope she's dead."

8

Good thing I got the P.I. license, Sara Flores thought for the second time that night.

Sara had followed the ambulance to the Barstow Surgical Hospital. She grimaced. She hated hospitals. The visuals were bad enough — frightened, desperate people huddled together awaiting word from harried, overworked nurses and doctors.

But the smells... to a wolf nose... OMG. Hospitals were full of the very scents most likely to put a wolf on edge. The aroma of fear was overpowering, and it made her want to chase something. Since she couldn't, she had to stop herself from pacing or from tapping her legs, or breaking into a run.

Then there were the raw meat smells. No matter how you dressed it up for visitors, in the back rooms flesh was being cut and blood was flowing. And over both those was the disgusting chemical stink of disinfectant. It assaulted her nose, and gave her a blinding headache.

Sara's P.I. license and explanation got her in for a quick talk with the doctor. She warned him and the nurses that someone had just tried to kill Lillian and was likely to try again.

An hour later, after two trips outside to clear her nose and ease the headache, the license gave her a tiny benefit of the doubt from detective Alberto Rodriguez. He made his interview with her appear casual by conducting it in a tiny patient-meeting room at the hospital.

Rodriguez had a face that made him look 50 or 60. There were bags under eyes which had seen way too much, and plenty of salt in his pepper hair, mustache and goatee. His body, however, looked mid 40's. He was trim. Sara guessed his weight at about 150 on his 5' 9" frame.

Sara found him interesting. He came across as low-key, not all aggressive as some cops are. But he had... weight somehow. Not a man she'd ever want coming after her.

He's been writing in a notebook, but he put his pen down and looked up at her with a cocked eyebrow. "Explain to me again why you rammed into her Jeep from behind."

"I didn't know what else to do. I was afraid. She was almost past the overhang, but she wasn't going to get there. I had to help her."

He wrote another couple of words in his notebook.

"You have someone watching her?" she asked. "You'll have someone stationed at her room at least for tonight? Because I've had about three hours of sleep in the past 40 hours, and I'm about to crash. Someone needs to protect her tonight because I'll be worthless."

He looked at her with cop eyes.

"Yes," he said. "We'll have someone tonight. So about this truck you say hit her. Did you get a license plate?"

"I couldn't," she lied. "The truck was heading right at her driver's side door. The plate wasn't visible. Look, surely some people called in what they saw. There were maybe 20 cars that could have seen it. They'll confirm my story."

Sara stood up. She handed Detective Rodriguez her P.I. business card with her cell phone number.

"I'm going to check on Lillian once more, then find the closest hotel and crash. Please don't wake me for at least six hours unless it's about Lillian." Sara walked away. She could feel his eyes on her back.

After six hours of sleep, a little refreshed, Sara checked out of the hotel and drove back towards the hospital. Her cell phone vibrated. A message said, "Call me. Secure." She pulled to the side of the road and fished out the phone Mason had encrypted for her.

"I found the guy who ran her off the road," Mason said. "But first — you have another problem. I put a tracker on your license plate number in the Oklahoma DMV months ago — as a precaution. It's good I did because someone just ran it. They got your address."

"It was probably Rodriguez."

"No, it wasn't. Two people ran it. I assumed the cop was one of them, but that leaves someone else as well."

Sara froze. She half listened to Mason talk, about setting up corporate ownership for her vehicles.

Would she need to move?

"Oh my god," she said. "Skidi. She's home. I have to get her." Skidi was her wolf-dog, inherited from the shaman who turned her.

"None of your house alarms have sounded. I checked right before I called you. But be careful. Someone really good could already be there."

9

Sara pulled up to the public boat launch — about three miles from her house. It was 8 PM and there were two empty trucks there, both with empty boat trailers. Both had local license plates she recognized. They often used this launch, so they were unlike to be the trouble she was worried about.

Maybe the DMV thing isn't related to this case? Nice to believe. But stupid.

She pulled out her phone and tapped into her home security. She looked first at the living room couch — where Skidi liked to snooze. She zoomed in and saw her twitching in a dream as though she were chasing something. She smiled in relief.

She searched the house cameras and found nothing amiss. She searched the outside cameras. Nobody was hanging around outside the house. Lastly, she checked the two cameras half a block away from her house — pointed in the two directions from which trouble could come. Everything looked normal.

She needed to get Skidi out of the house and safe — until she'd solved this case.

There was only one person Sara could call. One person Skidi liked enough to stay with. One person who could keep her safe.

One person she did *not* want to call. Bill Hanalho — a tall, gorgeous hunk of a man with long black hair you wanted to run your fingers through and a body she dreamed about. A man she tried very hard not to think about.

She forced herself to make the call.

"Bill? It's Sara. I need to ask a favor of you."

He was silent.

OMG, he doesn't think...

"It's about Skidi," she said quickly into the silence. "I need someone to look after her for a few days."

"Sure. Bring her to my grandfather's house."

"Thank you."

Sara disconnected as her blood pressure shot up. His grandfather's house! Where Sara had been forced to turn to a wolf. Where his grandfather had died, fighting the dead spirit of the man who turned Sara.

The very house where she'd first met Bill — only to realize they could never be together. He was now the head priest of the Lupiti tribe. He would need to marry a Lupiti woman, which Sara was not. And that wasn't the only problem. The man who turned Sara was the head Lupiti shaman. Shamans and priests were natural enemies among the Lupiti.

Sara shook her head, telling herself to focus. She drove to the street right outside her house. She needed to grab Skidi before someone came looking.

She rolled down her window and blew the dog whistle she kept in the glove compartment. The one humans couldn't hear. The one that told Skidi to come running.

From the couch, Skidi would have to run to the dining room to get out the dog door. Watching, Sara saw a blur of gray wolf-dog tear around the side of the wrap-around porch looking for her. Seeing her truck, Skidi leapt over the railing and down the front lawn. Sara barely lowered her truck's passenger window in time before Skidi came flying in and onto the seat beside her.

Sara used her phone to remotely close and lock the metal cover over the dog door. She drove the three miles back to the boat launch. After making sure there was still nobody there, she put the truck into park and grabbed Skidi. She petted her and hugged her and got a face full of wet, sloppy dog spit.

She was so relieved.

Then, steeling herself, she drove to the reservation. To Bill's dead grandfather's house.

Once there, she couldn't go in.

Bill opened the door and walked towards her truck. Towards her. Sara swallowed. The man looked better every time they met. He had a soft-looking denim shirt on today. Unfortunately. When she first met him, his chest was bare. Sara doubted she'd ever get that sight out of her mind. It was burned in.

She sat in her truck, watching him walk. She rolled down the window, and he came to it.

"Are you okay?" were the first words he spoke.

"Someone tried to run my client off the road last night," she said. "I was there in my truck. Someone must have seen me, because this morning they ran my license plate and got my address. I can't leave Skidi alone there while I solve this thing. I'm sorry to bother you about it, but there's nobody else Skidi might stay with and not run away. I know I shouldn't..."

Shut up, Sara told herself. *You're babbling.*

"No problem." Bill opened the passenger door and said, "Come on, girl."

Skidi turned and looked at Sara. "Go with Bill," Sara said. "Stay with him. I promise I'll be back."

Tears were forming in her eyes. This was the first time she'd had to leave Skidi with someone else. It was a claw in her heart, carving deep gashes. She patted Skidi's head and scratched behind her favorite right ear.

"Go with Bill," she said, pushing the dog away. "I'll be back."

"Sara..."

"Don't," she said. "Please don't. Just get her in the house."

Sara kept looking as they walked up to the house. Skidi looked back at her once. Bill didn't, thank god.

They entered, and the door closed.

"Aaarrrggghhh!" Sara yelled, gripping the steering wheel. She rubbed her hands over her eyes. She put the car in gear and got the hell out of there.

Ten minutes later, she pulled into a mall parking lot and called Mason.

"Skidi's safe now," she told him.

"How was Bill?"

"Don't, Mason. No snide comments about my lack of a love life. Not today. You found the guy who attacked Lillian?"

The phone was silent for a few seconds.

"Sorry," Mason said. "Yes, I found him. His name is Clyde Ruskin. I'm texting you his address. But he's not the brains."

Sara shook her head to clear it. "Not the brains? You accessed his I.Q.?"

"Funny. Not. I followed the truck on traffic cams — and FYI, Tulsa has a *ton* of traffic cams watching its citizens. 'Big Brother' is everywhere. I tracked Ruskin to a Hooters parking lot. Someone drove up in a Lincoln and picked him up, and drove him 10 miles to a parked Ford Bronco. I got the Bronco's license plate and his name when it stopped for the night at the house on his driver's license."

"And the driver of the Lincoln?"

"Not yet. He drove into one of the big downtown parking garages and hasn't come out. I hired a local P.I. who searched the garage for me — while you slept — and he gave me eight license plates for all the Lincoln's in there. I'm digging into the individual owners, but two of the cars are registered to two different shell corporations in the Cayman Islands. I like them best."

"You think he switched to another car there."

"If he owns a shell company in the Caymans, he's got something to hide. Which means he has a different private car."

"Good work! Keep on it. I'm going to see how Lillian is doing, then I'll go pay a call on Mr. Ruskin."

At the hospital, Sara braced herself for the smells and then opened the door. She identified herself to a new guy sitting outside Lillian's room — Officer Williams. He told her someone would be there for the next 24 hours until Lillian checked out.

10

Lillian's hands were clenched, and her one good foot was bouncing under the covers. She was scared... really scared like she hadn't been before. This time someone actually tried to kill her. Some crazy guy she'd never seen before had tried to run her off an overpass.

She wanted to cry. She was lying here in a room in Barstow Surgical with only one foot because her prosthesis was too bent to wear. So she couldn't run if she needed to. She could barely hop. Like hopping would work if she needed to move quickly.

She didn't have a single gun — they'd locked both of hers away in a safe. All those guns in her house — she needed them when her prosthesis was off. Like now — she needed them.

She had none of the security devices that protected her at home. Yes, there was a cop outside her door, but she didn't know him. She didn't know how good he was. Or how dedicated.

She was just lying here — like a sacrificial victim laid out and waiting. Couldn't run. Couldn't even walk. Nothing to shoot with.

She was helpless.

When Sara came into her room, Lillian unloaded on her.

"I can't even go to the bathroom without crutches."

She pointed at her prosthesis, lying on a chair by her bed. "This thing needs repair. I'm not giving somebody my house codes to get my other one. My neck hurts. They want to keep me until tomorrow. Somebody's trying to kill me, and I don't know why. I want to scream!" She closed her eyes.

Sara raised her eyebrows. "But other than that, every day is a trip to Disneyland — right?"

What? Lillian's eyes snapped open. She took a breath. She opened her mouth. Finally, she closed it. A rueful smile appeared.

"I'm sorry. I feel trapped and helpless here, and those are hot buttons for me. If I don't get angry, I'll start to cry."

Sara moved to the bed and patted Lillian's shoulder.

"It'll be alright," Sara said. "I'll go to your house and bring you the other prosthesis. And..." Sara leaned over and whispered in Lillian's ear, "We've found the guy who hit you. Do you know a Clyde Ruskin?"

Lillian shook her head. "Never heard of him."

Sara nodded. "Don't tell the cops, yet. I'm going to have a little chat with him first because he's working for someone else. We need to find out who."

Sara pulled back. "Doing better?"

"Yes."

"Don't worry — you'll have the leg in an hour max. And I'll come by tomorrow morning to spring you from this place and get you home. There will be a cop outside your door until then. Okay?"

Lillian's eyes were glistening. "I'll be good."

Sara turned to leave but heard Lillian say to her back, "As long as I'm home tomorrow."

Sara grinned.

11

Sara sat in her truck, watching Ruskin's house. It was solidly middle-class, like his car, but neglected. The overgrown weedy yard and a couple spots of peeling paint made it look like it was owned by a guy who cared only about getting drunk and getting laid — but who had a little more money than was usual for that type.

She'd already searched the place and found next to nothing. There were two receipts for his rental of the house — $1,075 a month. No address book. No pay stubs. No copies of filed tax returns.

Sara sighed. She hated parking by empty houses. Waiting. She was developing a low boredom threshold. She'd noticed it this past year. It was probably related to her transformation because previously, she'd been happy living alone for 10 years in a Colorado cabin.

She called Mason. "Can you find me a school that teaches driving for bodyguards? Aggressive training — driving when people are shooting at you?"

"I'll see what I can find. It sounds interesting."

"If you like, we could both take it."

"Maybe. I'll let you know."

Sara frowned. "I'm unsure about the other thing I need. Ideally,

I'd like to find a retired, top-tier Special Forces guy to train me. But I see so many problems in it."

"Yeah. Anyone training you in physical combat... You'd have to use full strength, and he would know something was wrong. Would you be as strong as him — or stronger?"

"I don't know. I'm stronger than any man I've come up against thus far. But someone like this? At peak strength? I have no idea. ... And I'm worried this would be exactly the wrong type of guy to learn what I am."

Mason laughed, a deep, delighted laugh. "You're sitting outside of Ruskin's house, aren't you. Bored to death. You always call me with strange questions when you're watching some empty place."

Sara smiled. "I do hate it. It feels like I'm sitting here, doing nothing to solve the case. I'm so bored I've even started to imagine someone's eyes on me."

Sara looked around for the hundredth time, again seeing nobody. Maybe they were invisible?

Mason's voice came over the phone. "Doing a stakeout beats working in a job. Doing the grunt work for some boss."

"Mason, I'm pretty sure that isn't our only alternative occupation."

"Well, not for me. *Anyone* would be lucky to hire me. But you? What could you possibly put on a resume? Wolf trainer? Vigilante?"

"Ha ha," Sara said. "It's only... Ruskin is probably out buying socks or something stupid while I sit here."

But Clyde Ruskin was not out buying socks.

At that moment — 11:30 AM — he was walking into the Barstow Surgical Hospital with a big bouquet of flowers in his hands.

12

Warren studied the woman — this Sara Flores — sitting in her truck and talking on her cell. She was parked outside Clyde's pathetic rental house, watching the place. Waiting for Clyde.

Warren had come an hour early for a 1 PM meeting with Clyde. He needed to be early so he could plant some evidence in Clyde's house. Evidence of Clyde's fascination — obsession, really — with Lillian. Evidence that would show Clyde acted alone when he tried to kill the woman.

But he couldn't do anything while that woman was parked outside the house.

Warren was watching Sara from the front window of a similar pathetic house across the street and two doors down from Clyde's. His Lincoln was hidden inside this house's garage, out of sight.

Warren remembered what it was like to live in a box like this — exactly like all the other boxes in the neighborhood. He remembered the embarrassment of it. The stink of it. Too many people all crammed together. Stinking baby diapers. Moms yelling for their kids to come home. Pathetic little flower boxes outside — as though flowers could make their lives not so shabby.

He shuddered.

Warren had rented this house through a blind trust after Clyde moved across the street. Just in case he ever needed to keep an eye on the boy. He was thinking ahead, as usual. Always two or three steps ahead of everyone else. It was why he now lived in a $5.4 million mansion, and everybody else he knew from those days were living in dumps like this.

Warren wondered whether Clyde had — finally! — finished off Bo's pretty little widow. Or had he screwed it up again?

The boy had always been both an asset and a liability, but his asset value had now dropped down to zero — whether or not he succeeded this time. Even lower than zero now that Sara Flores had found him. Clyde was the only link to himself.

But... how the hell did Sara Flores find Clyde? The truck Clyde stole for the job was stolen again from Hooters within the hour. Warren had checked.

He pulled out his phone and called Radar. The guy's real name was Jeff Sinkinson, but Warren got a kick out of calling him Radar like that nerd from MASH. He was a guy from Warren's Army unit in Desert Storm. A guy who owed him big time that he hadn't been rotting away for the past 14 years in a cell in Fort Carson.

Warren couldn't have turned Radar in without exposing himself. Warren might have gotten away with it — he was just having some fun. Extra spoils of the war on top of the financial ones he'd made. But Radar went too far. He'd killed one of the women, then another when she attacked him for the first killing. Yes, protecting Radar was one of the many smart decisions he'd made in Iraq.

Radar was tapped into security systems wherever Warren had interests. One of those systems was the parking garage where Warren kept his two Lincolns. It was unlikely this female had gotten even a sniff of him being behind Clyde, but...

He *had* picked up Clyde from Hooters.

He didn't trust Clyde to not run his mouth if someone else had picked him up. And he needed to give him his next orders in person. But protecting against one thing exposed him to another.

Warren pondered this Sara Flores. She was attractive. Her shag of dark hair framed an arresting face. But she raised a lot of questions. A woman P.I. was unusual, all by itself. It was even more unusual a job for a woman who'd never worked before — at least as far as he could find. Housewife for five years. Divorced with no alimony. Lived frugally in Colorado for 10 years afterwards, on her little inheritance from her mother. No job he could find for her there or here. Yet she now lived in a better house. Only a middle-income house, barely better than Clyde's. But she had paid cash for it.

His phone rang back. Radar had bad news — he'd looked at the parking garage video from last night. About four this morning, a guy got out of a car, and wrote down license plates from all eight Lincolns parked in the garage. Radar sent him a photo and Warren recognized a local P.I. named Joe Bob Rankin.

This was very bad.

Warren told Radar to find a way into Rankin's system and find out who hired him.

Maybe this Sara Flores was working for Rankin? He might have set her up in business to do some of his grunt work?

Warren nodded his head. This Sara Flores needed to disappear. But he'd talk to her first — see if Rankin was involved. Maybe Rankin would have to go as well.

13

Lillian was dreaming of Bo. She was in the combat support hospital, not long after the explosion which took her foot. She remembered the easy, lazy caress of the morphine — nothing was important. She remembered deciding to float away and die. Her life was over, but it was okay.

But there was Bo. Holding her hand. Petting her hair. Big, burly, scared-of-nothing Bo with tears running down his face. Telling her to hold on. Because she had a wonderful life to look forward to.

Lillian smiled, her heart filled with love, and reached for Bo.

Her right hand hit something hard. She heard a harsh, whispered, "Shit!" and the sound of breaking glass.

Lillian opened her eyes.

A man was beside her bed, but it wasn't Bo. This guy was looking at the floor.

His head came up, and it was the face she'd seen driving the truck which crashed into her. The man who tried to kill her. His name was... Ruskin. That was it.

Ruskin — who tried to kill her.

He saw she was awake, and he scowled — as if she were his enemy. As if *she* had hurt *him*.

Lillian opened her mouth to scream.

The man reached out and grabbed her neck with both hands and squeezed.

Where's my cop? Why am I on my own?

But she was alone. Nobody to save her.

Lillian couldn't breathe.

She realized with sudden clarity just how much she wanted to live. And... how much she despised this weasel. But he was a man. He was stronger than her.

Lillian's arms flailed. Her hands found no weapon she could use. She beat her hands against his arms. His chest.

No good.

He was leaning over her on the bed, so she tried to grab his balls. He moved his groin hard against the bed, blocking her.

She couldn't breathe. Funny dots floated in her vision. She pounded her hands against him, hitting everywhere. Ineffectively.

She hit metal on his right side, feeling a sheathe — with a knife in it.

Lillian grabbed the knife and pulled it out.

She stabbed him in the side — the only thing she could reach. It hit his belt buckle and skidded. It went into him, but not deep.

Ruskin jerked back away from her without loosening his grip on her throat. His movement pulled Lillian up into a sitting position and knocked her blanket back.

He slammed her upper body back down hard against the bed, and Lillian's hand opened.

She lost the knife. She heard it clatter as it hit metal somewhere.

Desperately she fumbled for it.

He squeezed even harder.

The world started to fade. Like she was going away in a haze of morphine.

No!

Lillian's feet were shaking. Her feet — both of them.

She'd put on her backup prosthesis once Sara brought it to her, and she'd refused to take it off. She'd needed it so she wouldn't feel so helpless.

The VA hospital prosthetist had shown her the makeup of her foot. Soft neoprene toes covered a titanium foot.

Lillian recognized she had no more than a single chance before she passed out. And then died.

She very much didn't want to die.

She twisted her body onto her right side and brought her left foot up as hard as she could. She had to bend her knee, but she managed to slam her titanium toes hard into the right side of his head. Right in the temple.

Ruskin lost his grip, swaying backward. His eyes blinked, and he shook his head.

Air! Sweet, beautiful air. Lillian gasped in lungfuls of it.

Ruskin leaned forward and vomited.

Multi-colored vomit spewed forth — all over Lillian's chest and her bed. She noticed the stink and the disgusting look of it — but only vaguely. She was far more interested in trying to swallow all air she could cram into her lungs.

Then, through the vomit, she saw the knife. It had fallen between the mattress and the bed frame.

Lillian grabbed it, the blade sticking up in her grasp.

Ruskin shook his head again and lunged at her — hands reaching again for her throat.

As he closed with her, Lillian slammed the blade up into his stomach. She ground the knife into him, moving it around.

Ruskin howled and bent forward, blood gushing out all over her. Joining, then covering, the vomit.

Lillian pulled it out and stabbed again, this time slicing into his shoulder.

He stumbled back, hands still clutching his stomach.

Lillian screamed. It was a hoarse, weird-sounding scream, but it brought two people running into her room.

She let go of the knife and fell back on her bed, still panting.

But she was also smiling.

She was *not* a victim. She was not helpless. She overcame.

And, oh heavens, it felt good.

14

Warren watched Sara Flores, sitting in her truck, get a call on her cell phone. The call was short, and it caused her to start the truck and drive away. In a hurry.

He didn't need ESP to figure out something had happened at the hospital. Was it good news — was Bo's wife finally dead? Or had his worthless nephew fucked up again? And... was Clyde dead or still alive? He called Radar and told him to find out.

Either way, it was time to rid himself of loose ends. Using the duplicate key he'd had made — again, thinking two steps ahead of everyone else — Warren let himself into Clyde's house.

His thin gloves looked like normal human hands from eight or nine feet away, but they protected him fine. Warren planted the evidence, then locked back up and returned to his watcher house.

Radar called with both good and bad news. The good news was Clyde was dead. The bad news — the bitch was still alive.

Both these women needed to be dead quickly.

Sara Flores because of her interest in his Lincolns. They could only lead to his blind companies, but it was still much too close.

Lillian because she deserved it. She should have sold her business to him.

Would Bo have mentioned him to Lillian? A funny story, maybe, about a woman — Janice — who dumped Warren for Bo? The woman Bo then abandoned for Lillian? Would he tell Lillian about the fight Warren had picked with him over it? Would he tell her about the lucky punch he got in that had flattened Warren?

Warren's blood pressure shot up. He slammed his jaws shut, getting the bitter-iron taste of blood where he bit flesh. He ground his teeth.

Warren didn't forget the very few people who got one over on him. They sat in his stomach, festering until he made them pay. Which is why he always tried to get payback quickly — because then he could forget them. Totally. Score settled.

But everything had happened all at once. The insult. Bo's lucky shot. That messy business with Radar. The end of Desert Storm. Getting his money back to the states. Starting a business.

Bo had slipped his attention. The only man Warren didn't make pay.

Two months ago, he learned — almost by happenstance — that Janice had died. He couldn't remember why. He didn't care. He'd had nothing to do with her after Bo dumped her. He didn't take seconds.

It's only her death reminded him about the one man who got away. Who turned out to be living for years — happily — right here in Warren's city. Worse — Warren couldn't make him pay because the asshole was already dead.

Then he'd remembered how crazy Bo had been about Lillian. Following her around like a love-sick puppy. Disgustingly in love.

That's when he joined the local Chamber of Commerce. He'd offered to buy the woman out, but she refused him. Then he figured to scare her out. Which also didn't work — and which apparently had sent her to the Sara Flores woman.

Warren's brain was churning. Both women needed to die, and Clyde needed to be the patsy. But Clyde was only set up to be after Lillian. And Clyde was now dead — therefore incapable of launching a new attack.

But... Clyde might have had a backup plan — in case he failed at the hospital. It could work — as long as nobody figured out Clyde was too stupid to have a backup plan.

Explosives could work. Clyde could have set them to go off when Lillian entered her house and did… something.

He could fix it to get both women. What kind of a bodyguard wouldn't go into the house with Lillian? But… not something that would go off if she searched the house before letting Lillian in.

Maybe… maybe it should go off when someone opened… yeah. That could work. And it would work whether it happened later today or two days from now.

Warren got into his Lincoln and drove to one of his storage units.

15

Sara leaned over the hospital bed and gave Lillian a big hug. "Great job, Lillian. I'm very proud of you."

Lillian grinned but shook her head in wonder. She had a small mirror lying on her chest and she showed it to Sara. "I keep looking at the bruising on my neck. It's half terrifying and half like a badge of honor."

"Winning a physical battle is a rush," agreed Sara. "Especially for women, since we don't expect it. It's delicious, yes? But... don't get addicted to the adrenalin and go looking for fights. Okay?"

Lillian laughed.

"Hey," Lillian said. "What happened with Jerry, the cop guarding my room? They won't tell me anything."

"He was injected with a big dose of meth — like Ruskin planned for you. Jerry's still alive, but they're worried about heart and brain damage."

"That's terrible!"

Sara nodded. "And they haven't been able to ask him how Ruskin got close enough to administer it."

"I need to get out of here," Lillian said. "I've been looking at the cameras Bo installed. Nobody's been at my house."

Lillian pushed an iPad to Sara. "See?"

Sara pulled up the recorded videos and looked at the active views. "Let me have my tech guy make sure nobody's been in this account making changes."

After an A-okay from Mason, Sara agreed Lillian could check herself out of the hospital.

Lillian waited inside in the mandatory wheelchair while Sara double-checked her truck for any explosives that might have been added while she was in with Lillian.

"I don't understand," said Lillian while buckling in to the passenger seat. "Ruskin's dead. He couldn't have done anything to your truck."

"Ruskin didn't originate these attacks on you — he was only the muscle."

16

It was getting dark, but Sara didn't want Lillian sitting in the truck, exposed. Neither could she bring her into the house. Not until it was cleared.

This protection stuff didn't work well when there was only one of you. She'd heard a rumor that Mark Zuckerberg had 16 bodyguards and spent $27 million on protection each year. She'd thought it was a joke. Or a sign of a bloated ego. But maybe he was just being smart.

She needed an advance team to clear the house while she stayed with the client.

Instead, because there was only one of her, she parked her truck right outside Lillian's white garage doors. She used Lillian's garage door opener she'd rescued from her Jeep. Then she cleared Lillian's garage, including the pain-in-the-ass drop-down stairs to the attic.

Sara opened the door to the kitchen and checked it. All being clear, she stepped back in the garage and motioned for Lillian to drive into the garage and close it.

Lillian stayed in the truck while Sara checked the house. But clearing the empty rooms didn't soothe her nerves. It should have.

Lillian headed straight for her shower, which ran and ran as if she was determined to use every last drop of hot water she had. Sara walked through the house, from one room to another, until she realized she was pacing. Her hackles were up, and she couldn't understand why. She'd searched the entire place and nobody was here. The locks and the security system were armed.

Finally, she called Mason.

"I know you checked it a couple of hours ago, but could you look again?" she asked. "Start with everything after your last look."

"Sure," he said. "But if your spidey sense says there's a problem, maybe you should get out of there now."

"I don't sense anything… It's just my skin is itchy. And I'm pacing. I can't make myself sit down."

"I say get out now. Why risk it?"

"It's not like before when I've sensed danger. I'm just uncomfortable. Please look at the past couple of hours and get back to me."

"Sara…"

Lillian walked into the living room, bundled into a thick Terry bathrobe with a towel around her hair.

"There's nothing better," she said, "than a ridiculously long shower in your own bathroom."

Sara smiled at her.

"Please, Mason," she said into the phone. "Call me back." She disconnected and put the phone in her pocket.

"I'm hungry for real food," Lillian said. "Let's see what I can cook up."

Sara walked with Lillian into the kitchen. She found herself right beside Lillian, as though they were in public and she was guarding her. She needed to stay close. To protect.

They walked together to the refrigerator, and Lillian reached out for the handle.

Sara's nose caught a few remaining molecules of scent — explosives!

Lillian pulled on the handle.

Sara grabbed her and threw the two of them far across the room and down to the ground, behind the kitchen island. She landed on top of Lillian, covering her as best she could. Her back was to the refrigerator.

There was a boom that shook the room and a fireball flared out searing everything in its path. It demolished the kitchen island, sending instantaneous ashes flying around the room.

Then, as quickly as it started, the fireball retreated back into what was left of the refrigerator and seemed to died.

There was silence.

17

Lillian awoke to find herself trapped on the ground on her kitchen floor. A faucet from her kitchen island lay in a blue puddle of melted goo. Flames were starting on her kitchen curtains.

She panicked and shoved off the weight holding her down and crawled to the untouched cabinet by the door where she kept the fire extinguisher. She turned it on the curtains and killed the fire, then looked quickly for more fire. The room was hot as a spa, but she didn't see any other flames.

There was a big lump on the floor she had shoved aside to move. Her brain scrambled the lump until she recognized the form of a woman. She was lying on her stomach, showing a bloody mess which had to be her back.

Memory rushed back in. She remembered fighting for her life. Coming home. Sara.

Oh, no, Sara!

She scooted to Sara and stopped, afraid to touch her.

"Sara? Sara?"

She was afraid to shake her to wake her. But... what if... Lillian moved closer and placed her fingers on Sara's throat. She nearly gasped in relief when she felt a pulse.

She didn't see any breathing movement from Sara, so she wet her index finger in her mouth and put it between Sara's mouth and nose. More relief as the chill of Sara's breath eased over her finger.

A phone. She needed to call an ambulance!

Lillian looked around. Where had she put her phone?

Then a phone started ringing. Right in the room. Somewhere on Sara's body. Remembering where she'd seen Sara pocket her phone, Lillian moved her body enough to reach into Sara's shirt pocket. She pulled out the phone and hit the "accept" button.

A male voice yelled over the phone, "Get out of there, now! A man was in the...."

Lillian interrupted him, "Get off the phone. I have to call an ambulance."

"No!" Said the voice. "Is this Lillian? Is Sara hurt?"

"There was a bomb in the refrigerator."

"Listen carefully, Lillian. If you care for Sara at all, you will NOT call an ambulance."

"She's hurt!"

"I'm her partner. My name is Mason. Has she got a pulse? Is she breathing?"

"Yes."

"Can you use the camera on the phone to show me her?"

Lillian did.

"I don't see any blood except for her back. Is that correct?"

"Her back is terrible!"

"I can see, but is there more blood?"

"That's all I see."

"Lillian, look at the phone and push the button for FaceTime. So we can see each other. Sara's life depends on you listening to me now."

Lillian switched on the call. She saw a handsome young man with Native American features and long brown hair pulled back. He looked very serious.

She looked around the house. It was hard to concentrate.

"Lillian!" the man yelled at her. She turned back to the phone.

"Focus, Lillian," he said. "Sara can survive this easily — she has off-the-charts healing capabilities. What she can not survive is going to a hospital. How loud was the explosion? Are your neighbors likely to have called it in? Will people be coming?"

"I don't know. Probably. What does it matter?"

"Because they will take her to a hospital. Sara has secrets that would be uncovered in a hospital. They would ruin her life."

"What do you mean? It's her life in danger here!"

"Yes, her life *is* in danger — but not from her injuries. I'll explain everything, but first you've got to get her out of there. Get her into a car in any way you can and drive away. Right now."

Lillian shook her head. "I don't know you. I do know medical trauma when I see it."

"You *do* know me. I'm her tech person. We've worked together for two years now. We've been working on your case. I first met Sara when she saved me from people trying to kill me — like she's been trying to save you. Now we have to save her."

"You're not making sense. I'm calling an ambulance."

"Only if you want to kill her." The man — Mason — rubbed his face. "Let me ask you one question. Then you can do what you think best."

"What?"

"You own the gun range where she's been training, right? I'm sure she tried to hide it but did you ever see her in action at the range? Did you?"

Lillian wanted to deny it — spying on your customers was not polite. But... "Yes, twice. The first time I was curious how good she was since she never left targets. The second time..."

"The second time," said Mason, "you wanted to make sure you really did see what you saw the first time. Am I right?"

Lillian was silent.

"Have you ever seen any human move that fast? That fast and strong and accurate? It isn't possible, is it?"

More silence.

"I'll tell you everything — or she will. But if you want to save her, you have to get her out of the house right this minute. Drive to some place nearby — where there's nobody around and no cameras. Then call me back."

Silence.

"NOW, Lillian. Or she and I will never forgive you!"

Lillian shut the phone and put it in her purse. Then she reached under Sara and lifted her to her feet.

She worried she'd have to drag Sara, but the woman's feet moved to help. Sara was walking, kinda, even though her head rested on Lillian's shoulder, and Lillian had to hold her up. Walking... even though she was unconscious.

"Lillian Knudsen, you are crazy," she said out loud to herself, hurrying Sara back to Sara's truck. "This is the stupidest thing you've ever done...."

But, in her mind, she was seeing Sara shoot. Sara had her back to the target and her gun in some holster up under her t-shirt. Then, in the blink of an eye, almost too fast to see, Sara would turn, pulling out the gun, aiming — and the target had another shot in the bull's eye.

Again and again. Left hand. Right hand. Different holster locations. It was like a movie — turned to double speed. Faster than possible.

Lillian suddenly knew what to do.

She laid Sara across the passenger seat, got behind the wheel, and drove off. The nearby Mercy Redeemer hospital had a big overflow parking lot that was usually deserted.

She'd drive there and call this Mason. If she didn't like what he said, Sara would be close to real help.

18

"Tell me why I shouldn't take her into the hospital," Lillian said on the phone to Mason. She was parked in Sara's truck as far from the hospital and from a security light as she could get while still in the hospital's parking lot.

The security lights were stronger than she remembered when she'd been here before. She'd sat in her car in this very lot, crying her eyes out after putting on a brave face for Bo. A couple of weeks before he died in this hospital.

At least with the lights, there was no problem seeing Sara.

She had hit "recent" on the phone, and "Where are you?" was the first thing she heard Mason say.

"In the Mercy Redeemer hospital parking lot — maybe 500 feet from the entrance. As far from the security lights as I could get.

"No, no," Mason said. "They must have cameras out there. Is it dark there?"

"It's dark, and I'm not moving. And if you don't quickly give me a reason why not, I'm taking her into the hospital."

"Okay, okay… is there a blanket in the car?"

Lillian looked around. "I don't see one. I'm in Sara's truck."

"Okay," Mason said. "She keeps supplies in the big toolbox in the truck bed. Grab her keys and get a blanket out of there. Not some clear see-through tarp. A real blanket. And make it as fast as you can, Lillian. Now!"

Shaking her head at the phone, she got out, climbed up into the truck bed, and opened the box. She got distracted by seeing handcuffs, a box with syringes, and a ton of dried meat. But she found a blanket and returned to the cab.

Lillian picked up the phone and said, "Now tell me. Or else."

On his side of the phone, Mason ran his hands over his eyes and through his hair. *How the hell did he...*

"Okay," Mason said. "I'm going to tell you something that's impossible. But I want you to keep a picture of Sara making those impossible shots at the range. Okay? I mean, if one impossible thing can be true, then other impossible things can be as well. Right?"

"Stop stalling."

"Okay. Any second now, Sara is going to start healing herself. She can do it, and she'll be as good as new. But... it's the way she does it. She has to change her body. Rather seriously. When she starts, throw the blanket over her. If a camera sees this, Sara will have to disappear. The government will be after her."

"You're making no sense."

Sara moaned.

"Sara! Oh my goodness! Are you alright?" She put a hand on Sara's shoulder.

Sara moaned again.

Lillian looked at her hand in surprise. Sara's shoulder was normal when she first touched it, but now... it must be broken. The bone was *moving* somehow.

Sara screamed.

Lillian remembered the phone. Mason had been jabbering, but she hadn't paid attention.

"Mason..." Lillian started.

Mason interrupted her. "Sara's going to turn into a wolf," he said. "Are you hearing me?"

"What? She's in pain."

"The pain will last only a minute. She's transforming into a wolf."

Lillian was shaking her head at the phone.

Mason's voice got louder. "Listen to me. You are in NO danger. She's transforming into a wolf. It happens all the time. It's normal for her. Her wolf will not hurt you. She's in control of it."

This is ridiculous, Lillian thought. And it might be, but it was also... also really happening. One of Sara's hands had turned into a paw. Her face was... actually... moving. Elongating.

There was noise in Lillian's ear, and she focused. Mason was yelling at her to cover Sara with the blanket. Saying she can't be seen this way.

Lillian picked up the blanket and noticed her hands were shaking. She threw it over... Sara?

The blanket covered her, which Lillian recognized was good. Necessary. But... the blanket continued to move as more stuff happened under it.

Lillian couldn't help herself. She lifted up the edge of the blanket to see. She'd always turned her head from car wrecks, but this... She couldn't stop watching.

Sara's mouth opened to scream again, but this time no sound came out. That was even more frightening.

Her eyes... Sara's eyes had always had these gold tints in the brown — like gold flecks. But now the flecks were turning molten. Expanding. Flowing into each other until her entire irises were gold. And they kept growing until they covered most of her eyes. Wolf eyes.

Sara's body jerked. Lillian could see her back crack and her spine reverse its curve. Her clothes were ripping off, and fur... oh my... actual fur was showing through the rips.

Lillian shook her head when the movement stopped suddenly. A fully formed wolf with compelling golden eyes stared right at Lillian. She was bigger than any dog Lillian had seen, with reddish fur highlighting the basic gray. The coat was full and shiny.

But the eyes... those were *not* dog eyes.

Goose bumps rose on Lillian's skin along with some atavistic fear bred into humans from caveman days — designed to help humans survive. Her heart pounded.

Maybe she should run away as fast as she can?

The wolf twisted its head, looking up at the blanket covering her/it/Sara. Then she cocked her head at Lillian.

Lillian laughed. It came out funny, almost hysterical, but... this wolf had just asked her why she was hiding under a blanket. Asked her as clearly as if she had spoken.

"Um... you can understand me?" Lillian asked.

The wolf nodded her head.

Lillian laughed again. And kept laughing.

I can talk to animals!

It was so funny. It was hysterical. Lillian suddenly feared she couldn't stop laughing.

The wolf put a paw on Lillian's shoulder. Lillian's laughter stopped instantly. Okay, that sobered her up.

"Are you alright?" Lillian asked the wolf. "Your back was all torn up. From the bomb."

The wolf looked up, like she was thinking. Then she nodded.

Lillian reached out towards Sara, then stopped. "Can I make sure?"

The wolf nodded.

Lillian ran her hand along the wolf's back. It was soft silky fur with no wound. No blood.

"It's a miracle," she said.

The wolf looked up again at the blanket and then cocked her head again at Lillian.

"Oh. Sorry. We're parked in the hospital parking lot, and Mason said to cover you because there were cameras out here."

"Mason!" Lillian fumbled around and found the phone on the seat where she'd dropped it.

"Mason, Sara's alright. She's... she's beautiful."

"Yes, she is." There was a noise that sounded close to a sob.

"Are you..."

Mason interrupted her. He sounded gruff. "Keep her covered with the blanket. Go back out into the toolbox and find a couple of dry packs of salmon or meat and a set of clothes for her. She has to eat to transform back. And she'll need the clothes."

"Do you want me to put the phone near her so you can talk to her?"

"She heard everything we said. Wolf ears are much better than human ears."

"Oh. Of course." Lillian put the phone down on the seat and went back out to the truck bed.

"Are you there, Sara," asked the phone.

Sara whined.

"You scared the crap out of me," Mason said. "You have to stop doing this. We'll talk later, but I'm starting to like the idea of you finding some Special Forces type for backup when you need it."

Sara gave a low, threatening growl.

"Forget the attitude," he said. "I always get the last word when you're in wolf form. And, by the way, Lillian is taking this pretty well, don't you think?"

Sara chuffed.

19

Sara plopped down on a striped beige and orange sofa, rubbed her eyes with her palms, and exhaled.

She and Lillian had checked into this 2-room suite at Tulsa's Brentwood Suites Hotel late last night, ordered a huge dinner from room service, and talked late into the night about werewolves and Sara. Then they both passed out for the few hours remaining before dawn. Lillian was going to stay here until her house could be repaired. Sara was staying as long as the threat against Lillian was still active.

The hotel chain offered a lot Sara wanted, including a 2-bedroom, 2-bath suite for her and Lillian and an adjoining room where Mason could stay — the man would not listen to reason and told Sara flatly he would be there in person. He was expected in a couple of hours.

The suite also offered dog-friendly rooms so Sara could get Skidi back. Without her, Sara was missing a piece of her soul.

As an added bonus, the rooms all surrounded a Mission-style interior courtyard where a guard could keep an eye on all the hotel visitors — those sitting by the big fountain, those dining at the WagonWheel Steak House & Bar, and those just walking through.

Sara rubbed her eyes and looked again at the hideous orange-stripped sofa, not to mention the mashed-pea green carpet in the room.

This was a real suite, and it was said to be secretly owned by Hilton but the furniture upholstery was very, very dated. Still, the sofa made her smile. She remembered sitting on something similar with her mom, each of them reading her own book. Good memories. Bittersweet.

The doorbell rang without a call first from the hotel. She looked out the keyhole, not surprised to see Lt. Rodriguez and another cop.

Rodriguez introduced detective Jake Sloan, his partner. He was tall, where Rodriguez was short and young to Rodriguez' grizzled vet. The sprinkle of freckles on his face made him look even younger than he was. Lillian came in from her room and joined them.

Rodriguez reported the bomb squad had found only the single bomb in Lillian's house — the one that blew when the refrigerator was opened.

Yes, Sara and Lillian agreed with him. They were both lucky not to even be wounded. Yes, amazingly lucky. They explained they'd ducked behind the kitchen island, which must have protected them before it shredded.

They handed the two cops a video from Lillian's security system. It was what Mason had called to warn them about — unfortunately too late. It showed someone entering the house 45 minutes before Lillian and Sara got there.

That person carried a satchel which looked heavier when it went in than it did coming out. He or she wore a hat with a wide brim, leather gloves, and a long raincoat. The only other clothing visible were jeans and cowboy boots — which could have been on a male or a female.

"It's probably a man," Sara told Rodriguez. "If you look at him by the door, he's probably 5-9 to 5-10, which is more likely a man. The size of his hands makes me even more sure. My guess is he's the guy who hired Clyde Ruskin."

"Any chance the time stamp on this could be wrong?" asked Rodriguez. He reached into his jacket pocket, pulled out a foil wrapper, tore off the end, and popped an orange circle into his mouth.

Sara tilted her head, and Rodriguez looked at the crumpled wrapper he was putting in his pocket.

"Tums," he explained.

Sara nodded, but then she shook her head. "I know it would be simpler if you could believe Ruskin planted the bomb before he attacked Lillian at the hospital. But... number one — the time stamp on this system has always been correct. And number two — if you looked into Ruskin like I have... the man was no mastermind. You might even find his picture in a dictionary, illustrating the word "flunky."

Again, Rodriguez questioned them both about any enemies Lillian might have. Again, Lillian gave them the same answers she'd first told Sara.

Then the detectives surprised both of them.

"Do you know a man named H.W. Caddel?"

Both women just looked at him.

"He owns Sharp Shooters and some other companies," Rodriguez added.

"Warren Caddel?" asked Lillian.

Rodriguez nodded.

"Sure, I know him. We're both members of the Chamber of Commerce here."

"Did you know Clyde Ruskin is his nephew?"

Sara and Lillian looked at each other. Both shook their heads.

"Did you know him when you served in Iraq?"

Lillian was startled. "He was there? When I was?"

Rodriguez nodded.

"I don't remember him."

"Did your husband ever mention him?"

Lillian considered, then shook her head. "No... not that I remember.

"When you met Caddel at the Chamber, did you mention him to your husband?"

"No... Warren wasn't on the Chamber when Bo and I were both there. He joined after Bo died."

Sara asked, "Do you believe he's behind this?"

Rodriguez shook his head and closed his notebook. "We suspect everyone at this point. If you think of anything — about him or anyone else — get in touch with me."

The men stood up, and Sara walked them to the door.

Rodriguez hesitated, then offered, "We can station a police officer here with you, if you'd like."

Sara said, "If you want to put one down in the lobby, great. But we're hiring two bodyguards for the room. Twelve on and twelve off. The first guy will be here in an hour."

Sara shook their hands. "We're depending on you to solve this quickly," she said, closing and locking the door.

Lillian had already picked up the phone. She was calling an event planner she'd used in the past, Judy Street. Last night she'd hired the woman to project manage repairing her house. Lillian wanted it to look exactly the same as it had — the way Bo had designed it for her. Except, she told Judy a guy named Mason Spencer would be handling the security systems replacement.

Judy had already paid off — she'd gone to the house last night and forced the police to search for Paws, Lillian's black cat. Who was now apparently being treated like a princess at Judy's apartment until Lillian could leave this hotel — which didn't allow cats.

Sara looked at Lillian, talking kitchen islands on the phone, and smiled. Last night Lillian had asked a ton of questions about her and werewolves and said she'd probably have more. Then she'd accepted it, like it was a new hairstyle on Sara, and went on with her life.

It felt funny, that kind of acceptance.

20

The hotel suite phone rang. It was the front desk calling to let her know Mason was checking in. And a man named Bill Hanalho with a very big dog(?) was there to see her.

Sara smiled at the hesitation in the man's voice when he said, "dog." There was something wild in Skidi that gave others pause. But Bill here? And Mason? At the same time? After all the grief Mason had given her about Bill?

Where was Scotty when you needed him to beam you up and away?

The doorbell rang. Sara looked out the viewing hole, and, yep, there they both were. Together. Two ridiculously good-looking men.

Sara shook her head. Mason stood as tall as Bill, although he was reed thin while Bill was more... muscled.

Mason was a full-grown man now. She kept seeing him as the college student he was when she met him, but that wasn't his reality today. His half-Lupiti heritage was more noticeable now that he was standing next to the full-blooded Bill. And, of course, Mason was scowling — staring at Bill. Not what she needed.

To hell with them both — there was Skidi.

Sara opened the door, and Skidi ran at her, prancing her paws up high on Sara's shoulders. Sara let the force of Skidi throw her down on her butt. She grabbed Skidi and rolled with her on the carpet, hugging her hard — which Skidi tolerated. Then she darted her head from one side of Skidi's neck to the other in a pretense of play biting — a greeting Skidi loved. And returned.

Sara wondered if she could just continue to play with Skidi and ignore the tidal wave of testosterone which had swept into the room with the two men. Probably not.

She looked up.

Bill and Mason were ignoring her. Mason's scowl was gone, and they were discussing their parents, siblings, and cousins — to learn where each other fit into the tribe. Finally, they appeared to have their respective families sorted out.

"So how do you know Sara?" Bill asked him.

There was a pregnant moment of silence, then Mason said, "We work together."

There was a longer silence while the two men looked at each other. Then Bill looked at Sara.

"Yes, he knows," she told Bill. "In fact, every damn person in this room knows. I apparently stink at keeping a secret."

Bill turned back to Mason, and some kind of look passed between them. It was a look Sara would never understand.

Men. Sometimes they're humans like women, and other times...

"Well," said Bill. "Skidi's delivered, and I need to be off." He turned to Mason and offered his hand. "Good to meet you."

"Same here," said Mason, shaking his hand. They gave each other another one of those men's-club-only looks, and Sara felt a headache coming on.

As the door closed, Sara went to the mini-fridge and got herself a Diet Coke, hoping the caffeine would ease the pain. Mason had followed her, so she held the door open — showing him it was also stocked with his Diet Mt. Dew.

Mason nodded and smiled. She handed him one.

He had two big rolling suitcases with him. Mason said, "Let me park these, and we can talk. I need to open the adjoining door from here."

Mason walked to a locked door in the living room, twisted the bolt open, and pushed the door open into his adjoining room. He took the suitcases in, took off a jacket, and came back in, opening the Diet Mt. Dew.

"Just one second," Lillian said into her phone. She walked up to Mason. "I'm so, so glad to meet you in person."

Mason smiled, and Lillian opened her arms and wrapped them around him. "Thank you," she said into his ear. "Thank you."

"You were very brave," he told her.

"We'll talk more later," she said, going back to her phone. "Judy?" she said into it. "The man who will be doing the security for the house just got here. I'll put you two together once we've finished. Now... about the kitchen..."

Mason took Sara's hand and led her across the room to the ugly striped sofa.

"Sit," he said. "Tell me how you're doing."

Sara sat. "You tell me about the bodyguards you hired."

"They're local, and they're highly rated. A guy from the Rez works for them and says they're the best in town. It's AAA Protective Services, and they have eight men and one woman who work on a contract basis. We'll have a guy named Kip Tarber here any minute now, and one named Connor Rockwood will be here in 12 hours and work the nights."

"Is one of them your friend?"

"No, he's out of town on another job."

Sara looked away, thinking.

Mason said, "If you don't like one or both of them, we can replace them. It'll be your call."

When she didn't respond, he said, "Sara?"

She turned to look at him. "It's fine. Thanks for setting it up. It's only..."

"Only what?"

"When I started this, it was just something personal. Something I was compelled to do. A way to pay back this extraordinary gift. And then you came in."

Sara took Mason's hand. "But it was still personal. The two of us against the bad guys of the world.

"But now... now it's turning into a business, isn't it? I mean, we have subcontractors. We need logistics and training. Maybe office managers. We even need tax accountants, I mean, *really*!"

Mason smiled. "You thought getting your P.I. license was protective coloration. But you're becoming a real one."

"Not just me," she said. "You're offering security system consulting. We're becoming a one-stop shop for protective needs."

"Is that bad?"

"No... I don't know. Part of me likes it. But it's not what I planned.

"And... I'm not sure it's smart to build up all this around a very big secret. I always planned to disappear if the wrong people found out about my ability. I thought I'd fly under the radar."

"Maybe that's first on our list — building you a bullet-proof alternate identity which nobody else knows about."

"You need one, too," Sara said. "And that would reassure me some," Sara said. "But... the more people we add, the more people we endanger. If someone is determined to find me, these people — you included — could be threatened. Held hostage."

"But... let's table this for another day," she said. "Soon. It has to be soon. But right now, we need to find this creep who's trying to kill Lillian."

Mason sat up straighter. "I've got a name for him."

"Is it Warren Caddel?"

Mason's face fell, and Sara winced. She should have let him have his big moment.

"The police are looking at him," she said. "Apparently, he was in Desert Storm with Bo and Lillian, although she never knew him there."

"The police. That makes things more difficult."

"Let's be optimists. Maybe they'll do my job for me and put him away."

"Sure," said Mason. "It's got to be at least *possible*."

Sara laughed. "You're too young to be this cynical."

21

Warren Caddel made the two detectives wait 15 minutes before his old-crone secretary Margaret ushered them into his office.

Warren smiled to himself when the younger cop's brows crinkled in puzzlement as she left the room. He was probably wondering why someone as rich as him didn't have a hot young thing at his command. In fact, Warren had several hot young things at his command. But he sure as hell wasn't stupid enough to let one of them get close to his businesses.

The older Hispanic cop was eying the room instead.

It was something worth eying. There was the top-of-the-line furniture — and there was the size. It was 15' wide by 30' long. Visitors needed hiking shoes to get to his desk. Along that trek, they would pass two casually left-open doors. One showed his fully equipped exercise room and the other his private bathroom complete with shower.

Detectives Alberto Rodriguez and Jake Sloan introduced themselves. Warren pointed them to the chairs across from his desk. Once seated, the detectives would find themselves in an inferior position. Warren's desk was six inches higher than normal, and the hidden platform for his chair was also up six inches.

Warren wanted the net result to be effective without being immediately obvious.

"Big office you have here," said Rodriguez.

Hmmm, thought Warren. "Big." Not "nice."

"I guess so," Warren said, shrugging. "I like elbow room. Now, what can I do for you?"

"We're here about your nephew, Clyde Ruskin."

"I'm still in shock about him," Warren said, shaking his head as if in disbelief. "I thought the boy was just a lazy do-nothing. I never saw him as violent. Well... other than the occasional bar fight."

"He worked for you?"

"Oh, no." Warren chuckled. "We paid him, but he didn't work for us."

Rodriguez tilted his head.

"My brother — Clyde's father — knew his kid was a screw-up. He made me promise him before he died that I would take care of Clyde financially. Make sure he had the basics covered — food, rent. Things like that."

"Very generous of you," said Rodriguez.

"I'm doing alright," Warren said, waiving his hand at the office. "I can afford it. Clyde gets — or got, I guess — $2,500 every month. I considered it an allowance, not wages. In return, he was to *not* show up at the office."

"You saw no signs of trouble with him?" asked Sloan.

"Detective, I hadn't seen him in ages. We didn't have any mutual interests or run in the same circles. I have no idea what he was up to."

Rodriguez wrote something in his notebook, then looked up and asked, "What's your relationship with Lillian Knudsen?"

"We're both in the Tulsa Chamber of Commerce. I saw her at the last luncheon — maybe two or three weeks ago."

"Did you know she was hit by a truck in the parking lot right after that meeting?"

Warren's eyes widened. "No. I hope she wasn't hurt?"

"Where did you go after the meeting?"

Warren's eyes narrowed. "You're fishin' up a very wrong creek, Detective."

He stared at Rodriguez. "I didn't leave the Convention Center until maybe 2:30 or 3. I got into a long talk with Rodney Watson — he owns Watson's antiques — and we lost track of time."

Rodriguez wrote in his notebook. Then he said, "You never met Lillian in Iraq? In Desert Storm?"

"She was there?"

Rodriguez nodded.

Caddel shook his head. "There were more than a half million soldiers in Desert Storm."

"She was supporting the 24th Division, which I believe you were assigned to?"

"Amazing," said Caddel. "I'll have to talk to her about it. But, no, I never saw her. And I would have noticed if I did. The women there stood out among all the men."

"When did you meet Bo Knudsen, her husband?"

"I never did. He was there too? In the 24th? Detective, we had over 25,000 men in that division. But... maybe I met him even though I didn't learn his name. Do you have a picture of him?"

Rodriguez pulled up a photo on his phone and passed it to Caddel, who studied it — then shook his head.

"Sorry, I don't remember his face either."

"So," said Rodriguez, "where were you on Wednesday, five days ago? Between 5:30 and 8 PM?"

"Why then?" Warren's eyes narrowed. "Is that when the bomb went off at her home? Detective!"

"We have to ask everyone."

Warren raised his hands in a 'surrender' position. "No, no, you're only doing your job. It's just damned insulting you'd even think I would hurt the little lady."

He pulled out his phone. "Let me check my calendar." Warren scrolled through a few screens. "Here we go. I was meeting with my head of security — Jeff Sinkinson— right here. Had a 5:30 meeting, but it rang long so we ordered in dinner."

"Thank you, sir. We'll need to talk to him, of course."

"Of course. If you've asked your questions here, I can have my secretary take you to see him now."

"We're done for now."

Later, in their unmarked car, Sloan turned to Rodriguez. "So... Caddel's alibi is a highly-paid employee."

"You didn't believe Sinkinson?" Rodriguez smiled. He pulled another foil antacid tablet from his pocket and tore it open, grimacing when he discovered two green ones inside. He dumped them in the ashtray and got another — this time yellow, thank god — and plopped one in his mouth.

Sloan shook his head at the ashtray, now filled with several green tablets. "Sinkinson was nervous about something. He's probably lying for his boss. But I wouldn't bet the house on it."

"What would you bet the house on?" asked Rodriguez.

"That Caddel knew Bo — and they weren't buddies."

Rodriguez nodded. "He was steeled for it. Controlled his face carefully when he looked at the picture of Bo. But his eyes..."

"Oh yeah."

"Funny he would wait this long to do something."

"We need a better look at his Army records. And Sinkinson's. I'll bet he was in the Army with Caddel."

"Tread carefully. Caddel and the D.A. are best-golfing buddies."

Sloan looked at him, one eyebrow raised.

"We need to be careful; that's all I'm saying. All ducks in a row."

Sloan pursed his mouth. "If Caddel planted the bomb, you think he'd be dumb enough to try again?"

"There was a lot of hate in those eyes."

22

It was now day seven of her hotel imprisonment, and Sara was going to start screaming at any moment. She wasn't sure she'd be able to stop.

The orange sofa and the pea-green carpet, which had reminded her of the 60s and her mom, now looked like the decor you'd see in hell's waiting room. It reminded her of burning fires, nausea, and puke.

She missed her house, the river which ran by it, and most of all, she missed being completely, blissfully *alone.*

Mason, the traitor, had escaped back to his home in Pennsylvania three days ago. She'd never before been as jealous of someone as when she watched him roll his suitcase out the door.

She could leave her jail — temporarily. She and Skidi got out for a run at least twice a day. The bodyguards Mason had hired were working out. She trusted them enough to leave for an hour or two. At least that was something.

The day guy was a big, bald-headed former Oklahoma University defensive end turned military operator turned bodyguard named Kip Tarber. He was in his late 40s and moody. Preoccupied. But he was also alert.

The night guy was Conor Rockwood, a Tennessee boy with the

remains of a Southern drawl. He looked to be in his late 40s, with ginger hair and beard, neatly trimmed. Sara had fun imagining it all grown out wild and matted back in his Special Forces days. She suspected he had looked very much like a movie werewolf.

Special ops guys in civilian clothing were not at all what she had expected. They looked fat in loose jeans and big shirts. The kind of guys you'd expect to see at a Hefty Guys clothing store.

But oh boy, they were *not* fat. Last night, Sara had seen Conor in a t-shirt at the sink, throwing water on his face. She actually froze for a minute before getting the hell back to her room. She worried her mouth had gaped open.

Lillian had laughed when she mentioned it.

"Maybe you should give him a tumble," she said.

Sara must have looked shocked because Lillian added, "He's single. Kip isn't, but Connor is."

Sara shook her head. "No thanks."

Lillian tilted her head. "Maybe you prefer that guy who brought Skidi back? I nearly got an electric shock from the air around you two."

"Not everyone has your rosy memories of love, Lillian." Sara turned to go back to her room.

"You don't get those memories by hiding out."

Sara stopped. She turned around and stared at Lillian without saying anything.

Lillian raised her hands in surrender.

Voice low, Sara said, "I fell in love once, and it was the biggest mistake of my life. Maybe I'll try again someday, but sure as hell not now."

She went into her room and closed the door, careful not to slam it. She leaned against the door and took deep breaths. The room felt like a cage. Like it was closing in on her. She needed to be running through the wild. With Skidi. Full speed, tongues hanging way, way out, to cool off the heat of hard-working muscles.

Kip and Connor both made her skin crawl with how hyper-aware they were.

Kip was the worst because he was there all day. She'd be reading a book and lift her eyes — only her eyes, mind you — to see where he was, and he'd turn to look at her. Every time.

As for Connor, she'd wake up in the middle of the night and slip to her door. No matter how quiet she was, the second she looked into the living room, he would be looking right at her. Did he spend the entire night staring at her door? Or was he that sensitive to eyes staring at him?

It was like living with two wolves, both from outside her pack. Wolves who were cooperating with her pack for now, who were supposedly on her side. But wolves she could never completely trust — in case they got hungry and switched sides.

Sara was used to being the top predator in any room. To feeling comfortable. She grinned.

Okay, admit it, she told herself. *Since you turned, you've always been "Top Dog."*

Now she was living day and night with two men who each considered *himself* the top dog.

Amusingly, she was making them as nervous as they made her. Conor had asked her more than once if she'd been a cop. Both of them tracked her with their eyes as though they needed to know where she was at any moment. They looked puzzled sometimes. They were probably curious as to why she set off their threat instincts when she so obviously was *not* a threat.

She grinned even more.

Then she heard the music from the Police's "Every Breathe You Take." It was the ringtone from her secure phone — the one she used with Mason when it was mission critical that nobody else could hear their conversation. Mason thought the song was funny, given his surveillance for her. And it was — a little. But it was still a stalker song.

She pulled the phone from her pocket.

"Great news!" he told her. "There's a tap on your cell phone."

23

Sara looked at her phone.

"This one??"

"Of course not." Mason was insulted. "Nobody could get into this phone. Are you impugning my abilities again?"

Sara smiled. "Well, if you're so good how could somebody tap into my other phone?"

"Sara, Sara, what would you do without me? Your other phone is our early-warning system. We like it when others tap into it. It lets us know what they're up to — and it gives us a way into their systems."

Sara rolled her eyes. Skidi came into the room and to her side. Sara head-nuzzled her.

"Okay, Yoda," she said. "what have you learned?"

"They want to know exactly where you are when you're not in the hotel."

"You know this how?"

"We disabled the GPS on your phone, remember? Well... it's been remotely re-activated."

Skidi rolled over on her back, and Sara gave her a stomach scratch.

"You're presuming it's Caddel?" she asked.

"Well... I can't directly trace it. His I.T. guy is very, very good. Fortunately for you, I'm better."

"I am oh so fortunate," Sara agreed.

"But unless there's some other really rich guy who wants desperately to find you, we're safe assuming it's him."

"Could he still be planning to kill me and Lillian? While the police are investigating him? Is he stupid?"

"Not stupid. But apparently highly motivated."

"But why?"

Lillian poked her head into the room. "I'm ordering pizza. Want any?"

Sara shook her head no and turned away.

Mason said, "I've been posting in Desert Storm vet groups. One guy says there was bad blood between Bo and Warren. He said Bo stole a woman Warren was seeing. Not Lillian — this was before she arrived."

"Is the woman still alive?"

"She died two months ago. A natural death — I double-checked. She had SCAD — a tear in a blood vessel in the heart. Apparently it's a little-known killer of young women."

"I can't see Warren killing over some woman. But... I can picture him killing some man who insulted him."

"You've got a choice," Mason said. "You want to stay in that hotel for a month or two while the cops investigate and find nothing? Or do you want to go out and have him attack you?"

Sara grinned. "You know me too well. I suppose you've already got an idea?"

"Yes, I do. Here's what I'm thinking." And Mason told her.

24

Warren Caddel put down the phone and stretched out at his desk. The calls had been made and both men had their assignments. That pain-in-the-ass Flores and Bo's so-precious wife should both be dead within two hours. Before midnight.

He would finally cut off any trace back to him.

He took a minute to place his hands flat on the fine mahogany wood of his desk and remind himself of who he was. Who he'd made of himself. How far he'd come. He took deep breaths and let them out slowly.

He opened his desk drawer and pulled out two Glock 17 spare magazines, and put them inside his jacket, in a pocket specifically made for them. Ever since the gulf war, Caddel favored the Glock 17 spare magazines for his Glock 19 because they hold 17 rounds each instead of the normal 15.

He patted his backup piece, a 10-round Glock 43, inside his right Lucchese boot.

He strapped on a belt which held two small holsters against his back — one accessible by his left hand, the other by his right. Into those holsters, he loaded two Taser Pulse guns, each with two cartridges.

He smiled. Bringing 59 ammo rounds plus four taser loads to handle two assassins was overkill. But overkill was how he'd stayed alive.

He hated using others for tonight's two big jobs. He preferred to handle business himself. But... he needed a rock-solid alibi while the two bitches were dying. He had to be out where everyone could see him.

One of the guys he was using, Kip Tauber, was new but highly motivated. The other, Gage Bowen, he'd used before. Too bad he couldn't use either again, but he had to cut off any traces from them to him.

And... he could always find new killers.

Warren stood up, checked himself in the full-length closet mirror, then turned out the lights. Time to entertain some clients at the most popular joint in town. Then, for a nightcap, he'd end up at the Goldwell Business Hotel, which nobody knew he owned.

Doing some "business" in his special conference room.

25

It was 10 PM when Kip Tarber got his final call from "The Man with the Money." The first had been two days ago when the man deposited $20,000 in Kip's bank account for 10 minutes of his time. Kip had listened — why wouldn't he?

Now, at 10:30 PM, he was on the roof of the Brentwood Suites Hotel with equipment that would allow him to swing over the edge and down onto the balcony of Lillian's bedroom two floors below.

A later time would be better. One in the morning was always the best time; people were at their least effective then. But the call said that Flores woman had left — so the time was now. He didn't really mind.

The outside lights of the building didn't reach up the twelve floors to the roof where he was. All in black, he would be almost impossible to see from the ground. There was a wind which swirled the dirt on the roof. It added a chalky taste to his throat, but it wouldn't be a problem.

No, the only thing worrying him was the possibility he'd have to kill Connor Rockwood. Not that he couldn't take him. He could. But he'd rather not — *esprit de corps* and all that. They'd worked together on a few jobs these past years.

He double-checked the device he'd been given. According to it, Lillian Knudsen was in her bedroom, like she had been for the past hour. Or… at least her phone was, he reminded himself.

But he'd babysat her for a week now. She never went anywhere without her phone — even when she got something from the kitchen.

He patted his pockets. He had a silenced gun in case she saw him or Connor heard anything. He had an even quieter garrote for her neck in case she didn't see him.

A police siren blared below, startling him. It started at full blast, then lost volume as the car moved away.

Must be a little jumpy.

He took two very deep breaths and exhaled. He didn't like this mission. He had nothing against the Lillian woman, and he half liked Connor.

He didn't want to kill her. Or him.

But… he needed to make the money *now* to support his family. He didn't know how many more jobs he could handle. His hands had started to shake. Not all the time, but at least a couple of times a week. And when it happened, he couldn't stop it. It happened two weeks ago at the gym when he was bench pressing 380. His right hand started shaking, and he almost dropped the bar on himself — he barely got it back on the support pole.

He went to a doc who asked him if he also had a loss of smell, jerky sleeping, and constipation. Which he had. The doctor suspected Parkinson's, which was incurable.

He could take care of himself. When it got too bad, there were lots of ways he knew to end it quickly. A bullet to the head would be the easiest, but suicide would nullify his life insurance policy.

It was all so ridiculous — he was only 42. Even more ridiculous to survive special ops only to die of this.

The problem was Cynthia and little Joey — who couldn't both live on widow's benefits from his military pension and the modest amount of that life insurance policy.

This job was worth $750,000 — half of which was already in

Cynthia's personal safe deposit box. It would go a long way to giving them a better life without him.

Kip shook his head. Time to party.

26

Turkey Mountain was Sara's favorite jogging spot in Tulsa. It had over 300 acres of rugged parkland right inside the city limits.

It was 10:30 at night when Sara parked in a big medical building parking lot on 71st St., then crossed it to enter the park at the farthest south side. If she parked in the normal parking lot, her truck would draw attention after the 11 PM park curfew.

The backpack on her shoulders would have surprised people with its contents — her compromised cell phone, a full change of clothes, a pound of beef jerky, two bottles of water, and extra clips for the Ruger LC9 she carried right over her tummy in an elastic band holster.

She missed Skidi — as a running companion and for her nose. Running was always more fun with her wolf-dog, whether she was in human or wolf form. But she worried Caddel might shoot the dog first before trying to deal with her.

In human form, her nose was pathetic, although still several steps up from a normal human's. Because of that, Sara lit out in a fast jog towards the wildest part of the park, the northwest. She wanted to transform into a wolf soon so she would scent when trouble arrived.

She jogged on paved trails, then left them for dirt and gravel paths, then finally left even those and moved into the trees and underbrush.

There was the smell of two unknown men ahead, but with them came the scent of semen and sweat. She sped past them, noticing them jump apart when they saw her.

When she was as far from the trails as she could get, she found a tree with a pile of leaves under it. She rubbed her hand under one armpit and then rubbed the hand on the tree, the scent would make the tree very easy to find later, even on a run. She left her backpack there, under leaves.

Sara took out the cell phone and walked to a pond about 40 yards from her backpack.

She placed the phone on a small rock at the edge of the pond, then took off her clothes and laid them out by the cell phone.

If only she could move deeper into the trees to transform. However, once she took off her shoes in a wilderness area, she had zero desire to walk on bare feet over leaf-covered earth. It hid rocks, roots, bugs, snakes and more rocks — all of which hurt bare human feet.

She looked up, wishing there was a full moon, or any moon. But it wasn't a problem. She could transform without one. It's only... once you transform under the moon, anything else is disappointing.

Sara had tried many things to distract herself from the pain of transforming. It was so sharp and so excruciating that she always swore she'd never do it again. But nothing worked.

What came closest to distraction was not to focus on *her* transformation, but on the world's. She imagined the world opening up, embracing her, baring all its secrets. Little by little the sounds and the smells grew and grew until the world itself was a symphony. The dirt, the water, all the insects and animals the earth sheltered — their sounds and scents all increased until she was overwhelmed, dizzy even, at the lushness of it.

Her last bones snapped into place — typically, it was her knees reversing to bend in the opposite direction. And yes, it hurt just as horribly as it sounds like it would.

Sara panted in relief at the end of the pain. Then she slipped silently into the woods on sturdy wolf-pads. She ducked down in a heavily-bushed area, with a few big rocks she could hide behind.

Her ears twisted from one direction to another, searching for any sound. She inhaled the air in each direction, letting the night caress its way up her long, long nose. Searching for molecules of man scent.

She had to assume Caddel would have night vision goggles. Vision was her most feeble sense — although she was unlikely to miss movement. If it was close enough to see.

She wanted to be sprawled out — looking like a harmless dog sleeping. But she also wanted the rocks around her — so he'd have to get close.

In case he was trigger-happy for any large heat signature.

27

S*even seconds. Not bad,* thought Kip.

That was his total exposure time from the moment he climbed over the edge of the roof until he'd secured himself and the rope to Lillian's balcony — two stories down and 10 stories above the ground.

He stilled himself and looked for signs he'd been seen. There were no changes in lights nor movements in windows across from where he crouched on the minuscule balcony. That had been the biggest risk — a chance spotting from a nearby building.

Seeing him from the ground would have been almost impossible, but he nevertheless checked it out. Cars were moving, and a few people were walking. Nobody was looking up. Nobody was stopped in the middle of the street.

The curtains for the sliding glass balcony doors were closed, but there was a small gap. He checked to be sure there was no dowel in the sliding track which would prevent the door from opening once he dealt with the lock. There wasn't.

Kip removed his backpack and lowered it noiselessly to the balcony floor. Opening it, he took out image-enhancement night vision goggles. He put them on and looked through the lens, through the curtain gap. The clock radio in Lillian's room gave off more light than the googles needed to paint a very sharp, although green, picture of the room. It was empty except for some end tables, a dresser, and a queen-sized bed. A shape was visible under the covers, on her side, her back to the window. It looked like she was cradling a pillow in her sleep.

Kip flipped up the goggles for possible later use. He double-checked his thin, black Venom gloves for tears, making sure they were fine. Then he tried the glass door. Many people left them unlocked. But Lillian had not.

From his bag, he pulled out a battery-driven drill already fitted with a custom attachment. The diamond-tipped hollow drill — large enough to create a hole his hand would fit through — looked normal enough. What was custom was the suction attachment inside the bit that stuck to the circle of glass and allowed you to remove it with no chance of it falling inside the room.

Once again, he checked the room and the bed. No change.

With his right hand, he placed the drill bit on the glass beside where the lock was. His left hand held his water bottle, nozzle pulled out and open.

He started dribbling the water down the glass. Then he pulled the drill trigger. He'd muffled the sound of the drill, so it wasn't as loud as normal. But it could be heard. His eyes stared at the bed, looking for movement, as he applied steady pressure on the drill.

Finally, finally! He heard the crack and stopped the drill. He pulled it back carefully, taking the circle of glass with him. He shoved everything in his bag and zipped it back up.

The bag would be waiting for him right beside the rope he could use to go back up to the roof or down to the street, depending on how fast he had to move.

After a final look around, he reached through the glass and opened the door lock.

The beating of his heart was just where it should be — mildly elevated. He was taking deeper breaths, and he had to fight a sense of euphoria. The world slowed down all around him.

The hit of adrenalin, the sharp focus — my god he was going to miss this.

He hooked a finger on the drapes. Positioning his body as far from his hand as he could, he slowly opened the gap in the drapes. Nobody else was in the room.

He pulled out his favorite double-loop garrote. It had two wire loops, so even if a person could block one of them — the other would still do the job. He held the garrote in his left hand and his Glock 19 with a GSL silencer in his right. Eyes carefully on the bed, he slid open the door.

Stepping quietly, he moved to the bed.

28

Sara lay in the bushes, waiting. She liked the half-rotted scent of the earth and the scurrying mice. What she did *not* like was knowing spiders and ticks were also there. Maybe already sizing her up for a bite. She wouldn't feel it, but...

Her human side recoiled. Shuddered.

She knew, from past experience, any bites would be gone once she transformed. But still...

She heard him before she smelled him — that was a first. The crunch of the leaves made by boots, no matter how carefully placed, was unmistakable to her ears.

Her nose identified one man. She spent another six seconds scenting in all directions.

Only one man. Surprising.

Sara wanted this whole case over. And she wanted to make sure Lillian was okay. Time for action.

She whined as a dog in pain. She got — slowly! — to her feet and tried to hop away from the coming man, holding her front right paw up as though it hurt to put weight on it.

The man came into view. He wasn't very tall, but he looked thick. He definitely had a bulletproof vest on under his hoodie. He'd dressed all in black, including his night vision goggles. His silenced gun was black too. He'd put mud on his face to prevent the shine. Easier to rub off and/or explain if he was seen here.

He was *not* Caddel. He wasn't anyone she'd met before.

Crap! Does that mean Caddel went after Lillian? Or has he hired out both jobs — so we still won't have him?

Sara whined again, holding her paw up as though in pain.

The jerk didn't show the slightest sympathy. He ignored her and continued his search. With his Glock 19 out, he moved to where the cell phone was waiting. Staying just inside the brush, he looked at the phone and clothes. And at the pond.

He didn't bite that she'd gone into the water. Okay, that had been too much to hope for.

Sara moved closer — roughly 30 feet from the man, keeping herself mostly hidden by brush as a scared dog would.

After he scanned the water and turned, Sara whined softly again and showed herself for a second or two, paw still held in the air.

The guy ignored her.

The man was either a dog hater, or he was well-trained enough to sense trouble. Or both.

Sara moved to the edge of the woods, about 40 feet from the clothes and phone but far away from her backpack. She lay down and began licking her "hurt" paw. Again and again. Acting like a normal dog.

The man spent 15 minutes circling the pond and searching all the brush, then returned to the edge of the woods closest to the phone and clothes.

Then he turned and looked at Sara. Stared at her, as if only now noticing her.

He started walking — slowly — towards her.

"Good doggie," he said as his night-vision goggles turned in all directions. Searching for a trap.

"Good doggie."

Sara stayed down, but she scooted slightly back. Away from the approaching man. Acting like he made her nervous.

"It's okay," he said, trying to sound soothing. "Good doggie."

He chose a very big rock about eight feet from her and squatted down facing Sara — letting the rock protect his back. His meaty left hand moved slowly to a pocket, and he pulled out some kind of protein bar. He unwrapped it and showed it to Sara.

"See how friendly I am," he cooed to the dog. "This is for you."

He tossed the bar right in front of Sara.

She looked at it but didn't move.

He again looked in all directions, then lifted a jean leg and pulled out another gun — a Sig P226. It used to be the gun used by Navy Seals. It wasn't silenced.

Holding a gun in each hand, one pointing to his front left, the other to his front right, the man took a deep breath.

"I've got your dog," he said in a voice which projected into the distance. After his soft, cooing voice, the noise was startling.

He must think I'm Skidi, Sara thought. *What an idiot. I have reddish-gray fur. Skidi is all gray. And I'm at least 40 pounds bigger.*

But he doesn't like dogs — he wouldn't notice.

Keeping her eyes glued to the protein bar so the man wouldn't suspect, Sara scooted a foot towards him and picked up the bar in her mouth. She sat up, chewing the bar, careful to hold her "injured" paw up to look helpless.

The man scarcely glanced at her, his attention and his eyes scanning everywhere else — waiting for human Sara to appear.

Sara considered her options. She could lunge and bite out his neck, but he'd die fast and she couldn't talk to him if he was dead. If you ripped out a man's guts, he'd die very slowly — plenty of time to talk. But the Kevlar vest he was wearing made that almost impossible.

What should she do?

"Answer me, Sara," he said, broadcasting his voice. "You've got 30 seconds before I start crippling the dog."

"Good doggie," he said to Sara.

He's stupid about dogs, she thought. *Good doggie, my ass, when any dog could tell he's tense and planning an attack.*

It was time to act. Sara would go for the biggest gun and hope the pain and surprise would keep him from shooting her with the other.

Hope. Hope.

His Glock-filled right hand was almost 90 degrees from pointing at her — the best she was likely to get. And, really, all she needed.

Sara's back haunches dug into the earth, the powerful muscles sending her flying into the air — straight at his right hand. Her jaws opened.

There was shock on his face. The hand holding his Glock started to move back towards her, but she was far too close and too fast. Her teeth clamped onto the wrist.

With a crushing strength of 1,500 pounds per square inch, compared to 750 for a large German Shepherd, her teeth bit right through flesh and bone. With a jerk of her head, the gun and the hand holding it went flying into the air, carrying with it a spray of blood from the man's now bereft arm.

Whoever said, "hope is a bitch..." well... hope didn't help this bitch.

The man's left hand moved right to her rib cage, P226 gun in hand, and he fired.

Ow! Ow! Ow!

Sara didn't know which hurt worse — gunshots or transforming. But it didn't matter — she never got to choose. Gunshots always meant transforming. Lucky her — she got both pains.

She turned her head and grabbed the P226 with her teeth, snapping his index finger out of the trigger guard.

She carried it away with her as she ran into the brush, looking back once. He was pulling a bandana off his neck in a rush to make a tourniquet.

Once at the place where she'd stowed her backpack, she dropped the gun, fell to the earth, and let the pain of transforming take her.

She never screamed once the pain of transforming took her. Not because she was holding it in. Sara wanted to scream more than anything. She screamed inside her mind with all the power she could give. But nothing came out. Sara suspected it was a werewolf evolutionary thing. They wouldn't have lasted into the 21st Century if they screamed when transforming.

But... maybe they didn't. Maybe she was the last werewolf on earth?

She shook her head. Sara took the time to dress in her spare clothes and strap on her Ruger LC9.

She walked back to where the man was sitting, back against the rock. He'd made a good tourniquet, tightening it with a stick. She sat down on a rock about six feet from him, her gun pointed at him.

"Good job," she said, nodding at the stump.

He moved his head to see behind her, then turned to look from all angles. He was looking for the dog. She leaned forward and flipped up his night vision goggles.

"She's over there," Sara said, nodding to her right, "eating some well-deserved steak. You want me to bring her back?"

The man didn't answer.

"Okay," said Sara. "Here are your two choices.

"Plan A — you don't tell me what I want to know, and I bring Skidi back here to rip your throat out and you die. Right here on Turkey Mountain.

"Or Plan B — you tell me everything you know so I can go after the man who hired you and kill him. That way, neither of us has to worry about him again. And — bonus points. You get to live.

"Your choice. And... in case it matters to you, I already know his name."

"Plan B," said the man.

29

Lillian's room was quiet as a tomb. Kip was halfway to her bed, garrote and gun in hand, when his spidey sense started itching. Something was wrong.

He noticed the shape under the covers wasn't exactly right. And... people who sleep with a pillow over their head should have a hand showing.

He dropped to the floor.

"There's no way out," a voice said. Connor's voice. "Lillian's not in the room, and I have line-of-sight on both exits. Toss your weapons up on the bed."

Kip figured he had just one chance to get out of here and remain unknown. It wasn't much of a chance. But he'd won smaller odds before.

He lifted his silenced Glock19 over the bed and sprayed the closet and bathroom doors. Then he ran for the balcony.

Not in war, but often in civilian life, a shooter hesitates at shooting someone in the back. Imagining the legal consequences.

There was the "pffft, pffft, pffft" of suppressed shots, and his legs crumpled under him. His body took out a side table on the way down, jarring his gun from his hand.

It was a pisser to be right about not being shot in the back — but to lose anyway.

Kip had landed awkwardly, his empty left hand not far from his feet. He reached the holster on his left ankle and removed his backup — a Sig P365.

"Sorry, Connor," he said.

There was silence. Then, "Kip?"

"Sorry," Kip said again. "Needed money for my wife and kid."

A black shape loomed over him, gun pointed at him.

"Put the gun down."

"Sorry again," Kip said. "Insurance won't pay for suicide." He raised the Sig P365 to shoot Connor.

30

Connor saw Kip's gun rise up from the ground.

He put two quick shots in Kip's head, then checked the balcony to make sure he was alone.

Satisfied, he came back in the room and stared at Kip's body.

"Goddammit!" Connor said.

Connor looked at his gun. At Kip's body.

"Damnit."

Connor rubbed the back of his neck. He moved his head in a circle, trying to remove kinks. Then he covered his eyes with his palms. He shook his head.

He hadn't believed Sara when she'd set up this trap. The idea that someone would attack Lillian when *Sara* left the hotel —not him — was...

It just wasn't credible. And, if credible, it was insulting. Because *he* was the threat here, not Sara.

But, hey, it's a job, and she's the one paying the bills. So he'd gone along. And son-of-a-bitch if she wasn't right.

He needed to call Sara. And his office. And the police.

He looked back down at Kip's body and shook his head. He'd never have suspected Kip would turn. He'd worked with the man several times. Kip had always done the job. The office would freak out over this.

"Damnit. Damnit."

He pictured again the way Kip's hand had moved with his weapon, moving it up to point at him. Requiring Connor to shoot to defend himself.

But moving slowly. Half time.

Insurance wouldn't pay for suicide, Kip had said.

But they both knew that's what it was.

Not that Connor would reveal it.

31

The Goldwell Business Hotel looked like many others. It had the traditional chrome and glass sky-scraper design and phallic arrogance of most upscale business hotels. It boasted lots of meeting rooms and suites where titans of industry could be catered to by their minions. Like Caddel. Who Mason was 99% sure owned the place, although he hadn't yet penetrated all the holding companies and off-shore trusts designed to hide him.

Sara stood down the street from the hotel, studying it. She was glad to be here and not at police headquarters like Connor Rockwood. She suspected he might be there all night, while she and Lillian didn't have to show up until tomorrow morning.

She shook her head. She still couldn't believe Kip had tried to kill Lillian. She thought Connor was making a sick joke when he called to tell her. She didn't understand. What good is money if you're dead? Or do special ops people come to believe they're bulletproof?

It was 2:30 AM, and the streets were mostly empty. An occasional car passed. One man scurried by, reeling a little, probably awakened and kicked out when his bar closed at 2 AM.

She wondered if Kip was supposed to meet Caddel here, too. Like the man who came after her in the park. Gage Bowen was his name.

Gage had told her he was to meet the "Money Man" after killing her. Right here at the Goldwell hotel. At 3 AM

Would Warren really schedule a meeting with two killers at the same time? Unlikely.

Kip attacked Lillian earlier, so maybe he was scheduled to meet Caddel earlier. If so, Caddel already knew he had problems — when Kip didn't show.

If Caddel also knew Kip was dead, he might still think he could control any fallout.

Mason wanted her to leave Caddel to the cops. But Sara was very sure he'd been seen in public by a lot of people the entire time she and Lillian were targeted.

Would Caddel have planned a meet with each man only to hand over the other half of his payment, like Gage had expected? Leaving them as loose ends who knew too much.

Unlikely. It wasn't Caddel's style. He wanted to meet with them because he planned to kill them.

She tried to imagine how he would have set it up. Caddel wasn't in Army shape any longer. Lillian told her he didn't quite have a beer gut — but he was getting there. If he owned this hotel, and if he planned to meet each of these ex-soldier assassins there and kill them, he must have a pretty good setup inside. Something that would knock them out immediately — so he could remove them and kill them elsewhere. Gas?

Sara was conflicted.

Only an idiot would walk into a trap where she could be immediately rendered unconscious — by someone who wanted her dead. Her wolf could be knocked out like a human. And killed.

But... giving up? Going home? It hurt her new image of herself. For the past two years, she was no longer a frightened woman. She was strong. Powerful. Capable. Like a superhero.

Good grief! Was that it?

Sara shook her head and turned away. She was no Wonder Woman. She was not bulletproof. Both she and her wolf could be killed. There was no reason to be stupid simply because she wanted it over.

She'd get the son-of-a-bitch, without walking into his trap. Not tonight, but soon.

Lillian would never be safe while the man was alive. He'd proven that tonight.

32

Sara crawled reluctantly into consciousness. Her eyelids were glued together, a dog was slobbering her tongue all over Sara's face, and the Police were singing "Every Breath You Take."

She looked for a bedside clock and was startled at first to see she was home. In her own bed. Then she remembered bringing Lillian here because their hotel suite was a crime scene.

Sara shook her head and focused on the clock. It was five fucking o'clock. In the morning. She decided to kill Mason — later — and pulled the pillow over her head, blocking dog spit and some of the noise.

Skidi decided this was a game so she placed her front paws on Sara and started pushing them in a jerking, "Let's play!" demand. The Police sang out, "I'll be watching you."

Under her pillow, Sara yelled, "Aaarrrgh!"

Delighted, Skidi jumped her full 90-pound body on Sara.

Giving up, Sara rolled over, grabbed the phone, and paused to come up with a curse worthy of the full extent of her hostility.

"Guess who just left the country," Mason said in her ear, once again getting the first word in.

Sara sat up in bed. She gave Skidi the hand signal to freeze.

"Tell me everything."

"Don't know much yet, but I will. Caddel's private plane left 30 minutes ago. The pilot filed a flight plan to Cabo San Lucas in Mexico. But... Caddel didn't use either of his phones that I'm tracking to make the arrangements."

"Okay," Sara said. "I need to be here today. Lillian and I owe statements to the police. But by tonight, I need to know where he ended up, everything you can get me about where he's staying, and how we're going to get me to that location tomorrow without the cops knowing I left the city."

Later, Sara and Lillian went to the police station and gave their statements about the death of Kip Tarber. Which were, basically, they knew nothing. They'd both been at Sara's home, making a home-cooked meal, leaving Connor at the hotel in case anyone tried to get in.

They were both shocked that Kip Tarber had come to kill Lillian. No, they had no idea why he hadn't killed her during the day when he was on duty. Except... wouldn't he have been the first person looked at? Whereas at night, nobody would have considered him.

Rodriguez said nothing to them about Caddel leaving the country. Since ignorance was good for her, Sara said nothing herself.

In parting, she asked Rodriguez how the investigation was coming and accepted his "fine" reply.

33

It was 3 PM the next day when Sara and Skidi prepared to board a very tiny jet. It was only six passenger windows long, and it looked like it could be tossed around by the slightest wind. But it could probably get her to Cabo. Probably. At least it had two jet engines, in case one of them stopped in mid-air.

It had flown to Tulsa from Harrisburg, Pennsylvania. Mason had rented it through one of his dummy corporations and was sending her a drone onboard for her to use in Cabo.

Sara rolled her eyes. She could picture how bad the drone instructions would be. She decided to not even try. Instead, she'd get Mason on the phone and make him translate the geek speak to English and tell her how to work it.

She tugged on her more prissy blond wig to make sure it was in place, then she and Skidi walked up the steps to the cabin. It was low, maybe 5' high inside, so she had to bend her head. The plane had enough width for two seats with the aisle between them.

Skidi began tugging on her leash, pulling her forward. Sara stopped dead and inhaled through her nose. Another passenger was in here. A man.

Another sniff, and she recognized Mason. What the...?

Since she couldn't see him, he had to be in one of the two backward facing chairs. Sara walked past him and sat down in the seat facing his.

The pilot was walking towards them, so Sara said nothing. She just cocked her head and stared at Mason. He at least had the good grace to look sheepish. Skidi felt no conflict at seeing him. She planted both her front paws on his shoulders and proceeded to lick his face with the same delight she would have shown for peanut butter.

When the pilot greeted her, Sara took a careful whiff of him — searching for the odors of alcohol, pot, and any other drug she could recognize. Nothing. There was also no smell of fear. He would have to do. She nodded at him and he returned to the cockpit.

The plane started to back up.

Sara turned back to Mason.

He raised his hands, palm out, in a defensive gesture. "Don't worry," he said, with a smirk on his face. "I'm not trying to trespass on your alpha territory."

Sara groaned. "You rehearsed that line."

Mason grinned. "Admit it. You don't want anything to do with setting up or operating a drone, do you? You should have begged me to come."

Sara grimaced. True.

Mason leaned forward, and spoke so softly even she — with her wolf ears — could barely hear him. "This is *my* job. You're disrespecting *me*."

Sara's eyes widened. She opened her mouth to explain, but Mason butted in.

"Don't even think about saying you were trying to protect me. I'm sick of it. If I hear it again, I'm going to throw you off this plane."

Sara's mouth twisted, and she smiled. "Well... you could try."

Mason kept looking at her. He was not smiling.

"Okay, okay. You're right. But Mason, my wanting to protect you doesn't mean I underestimate you. I don't. You also try to protect me — like being on this plane."

Mason rubbed his face. "It doesn't do any good trying to protect you."

"So... maybe it's time I realize the same about you. Truce?"

Mason stared at her, judging if she meant it.

"Sure," he said, although his stare expressed his doubt on whether she'd really change.

Then he pulled out a map of the Pedegral section of Cabo. "We've got a lot to do before getting back on this plane at 10 PM tonight. Let's figure out how to kick some bad-guy butt."

This time, he smiled.

34

It was 91 degrees in Cabo as Sara, Mason and Skidi stepped off the plane — exactly the same temperature as in Tulsa. But here, the ocean breeze made it feel balmy instead of sweltering.

Sara glanced at her phone, glad to see no messages. Putting it away, she turned to Mason. He was staring at his phone, eyebrows scrunched up. Concerned. He glanced up and saw the question in her eyes. He turned off his phone, stowed it in his jacket pocket, and walked away towards the taxi stand.

"Later," he said as he passed her.

They took U.S. 1 past dilapidated-looking small businesses with dirt landscaping. Turning on Lazaro Cardenas, the scenery turned to mid-level hotels and fast food restaurants. Further along the road, the restaurants got much more upscale, and places to stay lost the word "hotel" and replaced it with "resort."

The Pedregal section of hilly Cabo was for those who wanted action with their luxury. The multi-gazillion-dollar homes were all a short taxi ride to the marina or to shops and bars.

Mason used his blind corporation to rent one of the cheaper houses — only $1,500 U.S. dollars a night. Its two main attractions for Sara were being inside the gated community and being only two streets away from the mega-mansion Caddell had rented. His place cost $8,400 per night.

So this is what you get for $1,500, she thought as Mason accepted the keys and tipped the property manager. It was four bedrooms, four and a half baths, and 4,500 square feet. There was a covered deck with a fire pit over an infinity pool — with a great view out over the ocean. All the nearby houses had the same pools and same great views because the rocky ground rose high enough in this section to tuck in houses at different levels. As a result, most of the views looked like nobody was between you and the ocean. Even though that wasn't true.

"Your phone?" she asked Mason.

He shook his head. "Maybe nothing. Let me check."

Sara left one suitcase by the door, ready to leave. They weren't even spending one night here, although they rented the place for three nights. She pulled a big floppy sun hat out of her other suitcase to hide her identity, and to match a flowery sun dress and sandals.

Skidi was sniffing the pool, whining. All that wonderful-looking water and it stunk of chlorine!

"Come on," she said to Skidi. "It's time to earn your keep." They walked out the front door and onto the Camino Pacifico Alto.

For the next hour, Sara and Skidi walked up and down the streets, getting locals used to seeing — and accepting — the big "dog" as a resident. Just in case Sara had to make it back to her place tonight in wolf form.

When she got back to the house, she went to see Mason.

"So... what's got you worried?"

Mason spun his laptop screen around. A *Tulsa World* headline said, "Local P.I. Murdered at Home." The man's name was Joe Bob Rankin. His body was found today, but police estimate he died three days ago. All his fingers were individually broken before his death.

"Who is he?" she asked.

"He's the local P.I. I hired to get license plates from all the Lincolns parked in that garage. That's what eventually led me to Caddell."

They stared at each other.

"Well..." Mason began. "He had other cases. It doesn't have to be..."

Sara shook her head. "But it probably is."

"I got him killed."

"You did what you had to. If you'd waited, Caddel's Lincoln might not have been there. Then Lillian might have died."

"I know. But I don't have to like it." Mason turned away.

An hour later, Sara repeated her walk with Skidi, but this time her "random" wanderings took them to the cliff end on the Callejon de las Estrellas. There they got a look at the spectacle where Caddell was staying. While some of the most expensive homes were 10-bedroom, 13-bath, 12,000 sq. ft. monstrosities, Caddell had picked a home about the size of what Mason had rented — "only" five bedrooms. What made Caddell's so expensive was its height — above anything near it — and that there were no other houses between it and the ocean. The water was a serious drop down the cliff face the house was built into.

Sara turned around and walked down four other nearby streets which also ended in the cliffs. She was just a vacationing sightseer.

One hour later, she was back with Mason. The sky was almost dark. Time to go soon.

Mason was out on the pool deck with his two drones unpacked and ready. They looked like black locusts sitting there, ready to hop into the air to do his bidding. His fingers were flying over a laptop, so she waited.

Finally done, he looked up and smiled.

"Caddel's house has outside security cameras, which I'm ready to disable. In the rental documents, they swear there aren't any inside. I believe them because I haven't found anything else broadcasting. Although... Caddel might have brought his own?"

Sara's mouth twisted as she considered. "I don't think so. He's a planner. Cautious. Cameras carry a risk — they could catch something you didn't want them to."

Sara sat down on a chair by Mason, and again studied the pictures of Caddel's rental house from the realtor listing. She wanted a floor plan, but the rental site didn't provide one. Neither could

Mason find one from when it was built. If they were filed at some ministry in Cabo, they weren't in electronic form, so Mason couldn't get them.

Still, from the pictures, she could see all the rooms with a view. She knew where they were relative to the back decks and pools. Unfortunately, she couldn't enter from the back. She wasn't a rock climber who could scale that cliff and the overhanging decks.

They hadn't risked a drone during the day — the wealthy with their security minions would be too likely to spot one. As a result, they didn't know if Caddell was even in the house, nor how many other people he might have with him.

As the last gorgeous red lights of the sunset faded into black, Mason attached a thermal camera to one of the drones and sent it up into the air. High enough so the soft sound of it wouldn't be heard.

Sara looked at Mason, the blue pool lights illuminating his face. Flying the drone, he looked like a kid with the best toy ever. Enrapt.

Mason's face went blank. "Shit!"

Sara moved to him. "What?"

"Look." He pointed at the screen. "There are four people in that house."

Sara looked. Two heat signatures were in the front of the house, presumably guarding the front door. Another was on the lower deck — guarding the house against rock-climbing attackers? Another was near one of the two upper-level decks. The master bedroom?

"We didn't expect him to be alone," Sara said.

"No. I figured Jeff Sinkinson — the employee who alibied Caddell — might be here. The office says he's away for a week. But who are the other two?"

Mason shook his head. "This isn't good. They might be innocents. Maybe a couple of local girls. Maybe a Cabo businessman and his wife. Maybe..."

Sara squeezed Mason's shoulder to steady him. "We'll find out. Don't worry, I'm not going in with guns blazing. No innocents will be in danger."

Mason just nodded and turned back to his computer.

Sara changed into the second sundress she'd packed. Hopefully, it gave Sara two big advantages. First: it should lower or remove any sense she could be a threat because it obviously couldn't conceal a weapon. The high heels she wore — which she would wobble on — would also make her look helpless. Second: it should cause men to think of hot, sweaty sex instead of fighting for their lives. It fit like a glove and was cut low in the front.

The drawback was... the only weapon she could carry was a knife strapped to her inside thigh. She'd tried to make it a gun, but it showed. The dress was too tight.

"I don't know why I didn't just shoot the man on the street," she grumbled to Mason as she swung a useless pocketbook the size of a dime over her shoulder.

"Because you'd be the number one suspect."

"Oh, yeah. Good reason."

"I wish you could carry more weapons." Mason opened the door for her.

"I have you as my secret weapon." Sara tapped the earbud in her left ear and the microphone in both her earrings. "And I have my claws and teeth."

"Awooooo," he said softly.

Sara grinned and left.

35

The double front door of Caddell's $8,400/night rental was made of dark brown, intricately carved wood. At any other time, Sara would have run her fingers over the designs and enjoyed both the wood and the craftsmanship.

Instead, she took a moment to acknowledge the two different personalities living in her head. Her human side screamed at her this was the stupidest thing she'd done yet. Her wolf side had perked-up ears, a twitching tail, and was looking forward to having some fun.

Sara rang the bell, using her knuckles, and reminded herself not to touch anything.

A huge muscle-bound man answered the door. Oklahoma muscle, not Cabo-hired muscle, because the guy looked like a club bouncer who'd been too long on steroids. He was white and had buzz-cut fair hair. And a neck bigger than her waist. He looked her up and down and his hand, which had been resting on his gun, eased off a little.

Sara gave him a tentative smile. "Hi there. I'm Sara. I'm supposed to meet with Warren? Caddell? I believe he's expecting me?"

He looked behind her and, seeing nobody else, he waved her towards the living room. Sara could hear a saxophone playing slowly. Soulfully. Something recorded — her wolf ears could always tell.

"Have a seat."

Far, far in front of her loomed the absolute blackness of the ocean at night. An outdoor fire pit flaming red was like a beacon drawing her. Beyond it, the sapphire blue lights of the pool hit the infinity edge and disappeared into nothingness.

Sara memorized the layout of the house as she walked. A glass shelf divider holding wine bottles separated her from the dining room, with a huge slab of wood for the table. The bottles, broken, would make good weapons. To her left, low leather sofas and chairs faced mainly to the back of the house, where the ocean view would appear in the morning. The chairs and end tables all looked solid — they could knock a man out.

Sara smelled a second man, but she gave no hint of it.

"Oh, my," she said. "This is beautiful even without seeing the ocean."

She walked slowly out onto the lower patio, through the folded-back glass panels that left the wall completely open. The second man came around the corner from the dining room and followed her out.

She turned to him and smiled. "It's very beautiful."

He nodded but said nothing.

She turned back to look at the pool and assessed what she had seen. This man was smaller. Just under six feet. Not bulky, but... he looked and walked like an MMA fighter. He might be a bigger threat than Muscles.

She fought a sudden urge to look up for Mason's drone and wave. She hoped he was saving the footage. She wondered how she'd look to a thermal camera. Wolf body temperatures ran hot — 105 degrees. Would she glow noticeably more than the humans around her?

Footsteps echoed on the light marble floor, so Sara turned.

A man walked towards her. It wasn't Caddell. This guy was 5' 9" in elevator shoes, had a so-so face, and about 10 years of extra pepperoni hanging over his gut. She recognized Jeff Sinkinson — Warren's tech guru and alibi provider — from Mason's photo of him.

Three heat signatures were accounted for — which left Caddell.

"Sara Flores?" he asked. He did not extend his hand and Sara was grateful. If she touched him, she was sure she would come away with slime on her hand. His eyes had stayed on hers for mere seconds, then slid down. They paused at her boobs, then moved further down and stayed glued on her crotch. And stayed there.

And stayed there.

Sara grabbed his head with her hands and slammed it into her rising knee.

No. She didn't. But she really, *really* wanted to. He made her skin crawl.

"I'm here to see Warren," she said to the tops of his eyelids.

Without raising his eyes, Jeff said, "Ah, but he went into town on an errand. He'll be back soon. Would you like to wait?"

It couldn't be easy to talk to a person with your eyes glued to her crotch. You would have to work at it — to not raise your eyes even once. It would have to be very important to you to treat her like that.

Sara didn't know if Warren was actually out. If he was, then the fourth heat signature could be another bodyguard — or a civilian. Or, maybe Warren was the fourth and he had Jeff run interference for him.

Either way, Sara was pissed off enough with Jeff to give him a little of her time.

"Waiting would be fine. Do you have someplace a little more… private?"

Jeff's eyes moved fast to hers. He'd been staring at her crotch to make her angry. To play power games. His eyebrows frowned, and he bit his lip. He bounced twice on his toes and crossed his arms.

She froze her mouth to keep from smiling at his mixed signals.

"Sure." He moved to her with a sickly grin and put an arm around her. Far enough to grab the side of her breast.

Her stomach clenched — she was afraid she'd throw up. She forced herself to smile back at him. A delighted smile.

He frowned and pulled her tighter. Then he walked them out of the living room, past a full-wall media room that could easily seat 15, and into a bedroom. He closed the door, and the saxophone sounds disappeared. Even to her ears. Interesting.

"Have a seat." Jeff pushed her hard enough to shove a normal woman onto the bed. But Sara was expecting it. She let him push her halfway to the bed, away from him, but she never left her feet.

"How lovely," she said looking around. The bedroom door was solid wood, and it had a lock, but the lock was a crappy one. A bodyguard could kick it in. She inhaled, searching for scents. There was nobody else in the room. She didn't smell a gun, either, but in human form she was only 50/50 in catching its much fainter gun-oil scent.

"Jeff," she said, walking back to him. She forced herself to put a hand on his chest and trailed it over him as she walked behind him, closing, letting him smell her perfume. Her right hand came over his shoulder and rubbed down his chest.

She could stand it. Just barely. Because...

She jerked her arm up, catching his throat in the "V" of her elbow, shutting off the blood flow on each side of his neck. She lifted his feet off the floor as she squeezed.

It never got old — having superior strength.

He struggled, hands punching at her, legs kicking. He tried to yell, but he didn't have the air to do so. It was 14 long years since Jeff had passed basic training — and that must have been his last time in the vicinity of a gym. He also had no fighting skills.

Twelve seconds later, he was out cold.

Sara threw him on the bed. She removed her super-thin gloves from her bra and put them on. Then she patted him down and removed his weapons. He had a red Balisong knife in his pants pocket and the strangest mini-revolver she'd ever seen strapped to his ankle. It was Stainless steel with a tarted-up fancy wood handle and no trigger guard whatsoever. Too bad he was carrying it in his boot and not in a front pants pocket — where it might have gone off accidentally.

She sniffed the gun. He wasn't taking good care of it — he hadn't oiled it in, maybe, forever.

Sara grabbed a washcloth from the attached bath and removed a cover from one of the bed pillows. She crammed the washcloth in his mouth and tied the pillow cover around his head, tightly holding the washcloth inside his jaws.

There were two bedside table lamps, so she pulled her knife from her thigh holster and cut the electric cords from both. One she used to tie his hands behind him. The other tied his ankles together.

He was still out, so she walked back to the door, locked it, and slid a chair back up under the doorknob, jamming it tight.

She put the funny gun in a bedside table drawer and flushed its two bullets down the toilet. Her knife went back in its holster on her upper thigh. She kept Jeff's knife out.

From the bed came grunts, groans, and thrashing. Sara turned back to Jeff and showed him his Balisong. She put a finger to her lips and shook her head slowly — all the while twisting the knife back and forth.

Back and forth.

Jeff shut up.

She touched one of her microphone earrings. "Update," she said. "Where are they?"

Jeff's brows scrunched, and he shook his head in confusion.

Sara had a moment's panic as she considered whether the soundproofing would affect... finally, Mason's voice came in her ear. "One in the room with you. One at the front door. Two by the deck. Can't confirm if one is Warren."

"Alert me if one comes towards me or if a new person arrives."

Jeff watched her. He was listening. Sara saw his eyes growing wider.

She grabbed the second chair in the room, pulled it close to the bed, and sat down. Within easy cutting distance of Jeff. Knife held at the ready.

"So, Jeff, I'm curious. Why would a man who's skilled with computers work for — and lie for — a man like Warren? Is it only for the money?"

Jeff's eyes slid away.

"No. I didn't think so."

She tapped him on the chest with the knife.

Mason's voice interrupted her. "A Range Rover is approaching. I see a driver and someone in the back. One second."

Sara waited.

"Entering the house garage. That makes six of them and one of you. Time to get out of there."

36

"Five of them," Sara said to Mason. "This one's out of commission for a while."

She picked up one of the table lamps she'd ruined and hit Jeff on the side of the head with the base. He should be out for at least 30 minutes. Then she dragged his hog-tied, gagged body into the attached bath and closed the door on him. His Balisong she threw under the bed.

Sara checked herself in the mirror. She tugged her blond pouffy wig back in place and patted her knife on her thigh. She removed the chair from the doorknob, unlocked the door, and walked out.

She walked into the living room as Warren and another man came into the dining room.

Warren stopped. She did too.

"Well, well," he said. "Sara Flores. I wondered if you'd come down here."

"I thought it was time we meet, don't you?"

"Absolutely."

Warren turned to the man beside him. "Steve, change of plans. Go back to the car. I'll be there in a couple of minutes."

Steve raised his eyebrows. Warren's face didn't move at all. Nodding, Steve turned and retraced his steps.

Warren waited for his driver to leave, then nodded at the MMA bodyguard to follow him.

Sara smiled. Just Warren and Muscles were the room with her right now. But… where was that sixth heat signature?

Warren walked closer to her. "I had so many questions I wanted to ask you."

Sara's smile grew.

"But what does it matter? It's long past time you were dead."

Warren pulled out a black automatic and shot Sara dead center.

The impact pushed her back. The back of her knees hit the edge of the white leather sofa and she fell on it.

Son-of-a-bitch — it hurts!

Warren came closer. About five feet away. He pointed his gun at Sara's head.

Oh, hell no! Who knows if I can survive that?

Sara leaned forward, kicking against the sofa to add power, and flew straight into Warren's knees. They made loud cracking noises as they broke. It knocked both of them down to a gorgeous Mayan rug, but Caddell rolled on top.

Her entire body ached with the need — the compulsion — to change to a wolf. She clamped down tight on that need, allowing only her left arm to turn into a paw.

And claws.

Sara slashed her claws across Warren's carotid artery, causing a hot spray of blood to gush over her. He fell back off her, gurgled, and clamped his hands on his throat in a desperate attempt to save his life.

"Idiot," she told him. "If you'd only left Lillian alone…"

Muscles! She turned quickly to find him standing stock still, ten feet away, staring at… Staring at her left paw.

He jerked out of his trance.

Sara grabbed the knife from her thigh.

Muscles pulled out his gun.

Sara threw the knife, then dove — trying to get behind the sofa.

Muscles pulled the trigger.

The knife buried itself in his right shoulder.

The bullet winged Sara as she dove. She screamed. The need in her to transform was now almost overpowering. She screamed to hold it back. Then she reconsidered.

Fuck it. He wants it? He can have it.

She continued screaming until the transformation shut off her vocal cords. Her arms and legs completed their transition to paws. Fur rippled out and covered her body. Her nose and mouth left her face and moved forward. Far forward. Her human teeth elongated, and her gums bled as 10 more teeth broke out. Finally, the worst pain of all was the crack of her spine as it reversed shape.

A minute after it started, she rose up from behind the couch, resting her front paws on it. She was 130 pounds of pissed-off wolf.

Sara lifted her front lip and growled at Muscles.

His eyes were huge, white showing all around the blue. He'd moved his gun to his left hand, but it just hung there.

His right made the sign of a cross over his chest.

Sara opened her jaws.

Muscles turned and ran.

A gasp sounded behind her, and Sara turned quickly. MMA man had come back to the living room, drawn here undoubtedly by the gunshot. He was 15 feet from her, skidding to a stop, when Sara launched herself at him.

It wasn't until she was airborne that she questioned whether she could reach him in one jump.

Fortunately...

She opened her jaws, aiming for his neck, but his shoulder blocked a killing bite, and the momentum tumbled them both hard on the floor. She opened her jaws, got a better grip on his neck, then bit hard — snapping his spine. His struggles stopped instantly.

Sara was completely covered in hot blood. She smelled another man and jerked her head around. The driver was standing there, mouth gaping open.

She wrinkled her nose, displaying her very-bloody, very-long teeth. Growling. The driver raised his hands and backed slowly out of the room. A minute later, she heard a car start and drive away.

Where was that sixth heat signature?

Sara padded on wolf feet through the house, her claws clicking on the marble floors. Jeff was where she'd left him, tied up in the tub. She finally found the smell of a woman on the top floor behind one of the bedroom doors.

There was a key sticking in the door knob of the room, the only one she'd seen in the house. Sara stood on her hind paws and wrapped her front paw pads around the doorknob to open it. It wouldn't turn.

The woman was locked in. That meant she couldn't have possibly caused the mess out in the living room. No risk to her from the cops.

It was time to go. Smarter to go in her current form than to have a woman seen walking from this charnel house.

Sara went to one of the two pool decks on the upper floor. She made sure it had steps, not just a rung, and dove into the pool, washing all the blood away. She padded up the pool steps and gave herself a big full-body shake to dry off her fur.

She looked up into the night sky and waved a paw to reassure Mason. Then she walked out the open garage door.

A nice doggy on her way home after a little walk.

37

One week later, at 8 PM, Sara walked into BK's Shooting Range. It had been closed for more than a week now, but Lillian planned to reopen it the next morning.

Wine glasses, bubbly, and a plate full of roast beef sandwiches were spread out on the large glass counter where shooters paid. The rest of the waiting room had small sofas, a bunch of chairs and three coffee tables.

Mason was already there, feet up on one of the tables, chatting with Judy Street — the woman who'd worked miracles to get Lillian's kitchen ready enough that she could move back while the work continued. Connor Rockwood was there as well, wandering around the place, looking at everything.

Lillian had a big smile on her face as she popped a cork from some French bottle of champagne and splashed it into glasses for them all.

"A toast," she said as everyone gathered around. "To nobody wanting to kill me any more."

"Here, here," said Mason.

"I'll drink to that," said Judy.

"And thanks to you," Lillian said, nodding at Sara. "For everything."

"But I didn't..."

"No," said Lillian. "You do not get to disagree. This is my party. Say, 'You're welcome,' drink your bubbly, and shut up."

Sara smiled. "You're welcome."

Paws was there. Half hidden behind a counter. Staring at Sara. Lillian saw her and frowned.

"I don't know why..." Lillian smiled and nodded her head. "I guess now I *do* know why she reacts that way to you."

Sara smiled most of the night. She'd never before had a little after-action celebration. She decided she liked it.

She knew she needed to stay far from Detective Rodriguez for the foreseeable future. He was bothered by Caddell being killed by a wild dog while staying at a Mexican resort. Sara knew that because he had personally interviewed the pizza delivery man who came to Sara's house and handed two large pizzas directly to Connor right about the time Caddell was dying.

Rodriguez had also interviewed Judy Street. Judy told him she'd met with Lillian at the house a couple hours before the pizza man arrived and stayed for dinner.

Lillian told Rodriguez she'd looked into my room to see if I wanted pizza, but I was sleeping soundly.

Sara shook it off. *It's over. Lillian is safe. Time to move on.*

She turned to watch Judy flirt with the men. Judy was a 55-year-old girly girl with straight but tousled gray hair framing her face. She looked good. Everyone loved her — unless you were a contractor running behind on a project. Then she was your worst enemy.

Sara watched her tease Mason — at one point getting a blush out of him. That made her grin. Mason planned to offer Judy some remote-work jobs — he was fed up with all the admin stuff he'd been doing for them.

Connor was sticking close to Lillian. The two of them kept glancing at each other when they thought nobody was looking. That also made Sara smile.

About 10 PM she found herself talking to Connor. She'd been uncomfortable having him at her house and even more uncomfortable worrying he would notice she wasn't in the house most of the afternoon and night when Caddell died.

She made a mental note to herself to have another talk with Lillian about protecting her secret. If she and Conner got serious about each other... Sara had a hard time trusting anyone. She hadn't been that way as a child, but she'd learned distrust during her five-year marriage.

She asked Connor if he was committed to full-time bodyguard work. He said he was considering cutting back to the occasional job. He wanted to figure out what else he might like to do.

"After all, I'm in my 40's," he lied. But 50 was close enough, wasn't it? "I won't be this strong — or this handsome — forever."

Sara grinned. Then she caught Mason staring at her, nodding at Connor. She rolled her eyes at Mason.

Connor raised an eyebrow in question. Sara hesitated.

Oh, hell, she thought. *You know you're going to do it eventually, so might as well do it now.*

"I might want to hire you myself for some training."

"What kind of training?"

"I'd like to learn more about mounting rescue operations. Learn what you know about them. And... learn how you were trained to fight."

Connor tilted his head at her.

"I'm a good shot, I'm strong, and I'm motivated. But I never learned tactics. It would help me in my private eye work."

Connor studied her. "It's a lot to learn. You might prefer one of those self-defense classes."

"No, I want to learn much more than that. Let's give it a try. I think you might be very surprised."

~

CONNOR *IS* SURPRISED, but so is Sara on her next case. A simple missing woman turns into something much more deadly as a billionaire scumbag threatens Sara and her team. Grab your copy of 192 Days Missing — Book 2 in the Sara Flores, Werewolf P.I. series.

WolfLady.net

SNEAK PEAK AT THE NEXT NOVEL

SARA FLORES, WEREWOLF P.I. SERIES

Prologue

192 Days Earlier
Lupiti, Oklahoma

Alaska Brown no longer noticed all the security cameras at Tulsa's Four Leaf Clover Casino. She knew they were in the parking lot where she parked, in the cashier's cage where she worked, and in the casino restaurant where she got dinner. That didn't even count the five cameras each at the many, many gaming tables.

As far as she knew, the only place on casino property without cameras was inside the bathrooms.

She believed they'd have cameras there, too, if it weren't illegal.

She awakened at 11:30 that morning, the 17th of September, as though it were a normal day instead of what was to become the worst day of her life.

She looked outside and saw the thermometer showing 81 degrees, which made her smile. Finally — a little relief from what had been a brutal summer.

She checked to make sure her daughter Macey had left for high school and winced at the clothes Macey had left strewn on her bed. She told herself to leave them — Macey needed to learn responsibility. But... "Maybe next time," she said as she picked them up and put them back on hangers.

She opened the door to Ricky's room and gave a short sigh. He wouldn't be home from college until Thanksgiving — which seemed years away. She made a mental note to look for a book he'd like when she had her dinner break. She could send it to him.

Alaska started two cups of coffee brewing, then stared at her wardrobe. She only had two suits, so she switched them each day. Yesterday was the yellow one, so today it would have to be the blue one. But she paired it with a pink blouse instead of the white she wore two days ago.

She tightened her mouth. She needed to look professional so she got that promotion her boss was dangling. But he always dressed so sharp and she'd seen him noticing how she dressed. Maybe she needed to find the money — somehow — for another suit?

Alaska downed one cup of coffee — half sugar — before putting on her makeup. She poured the second cup in her to-go mug for her trip into Tulsa. The drive time wasn't wasted — she always used it to talk to her mom. To make sure she and dad were doing okay. It was the "special treat" part of her day.

Her shift in the cashiers' cage ended at 10 PM that night, as usual. As she stepped into the exit elevator for the parking lot, Alaska assumed cameras were still following her.

As the doors were closing, a gorgeous young woman jumped in. She had long black hair and looked a little like Alaska's daughter Macey. Alaska nodded at her. She'd seen the girl a few times and knew she worked as a cocktail server.

Alaska followed her out onto the fourth parking level, but stopped when she saw the girl looking around, confused. She was staring at the letters and numbers on the columns and looking down at her phone.

"Do you know where you're parked?" Alaska asked her.

The girl shook her head. "My boyfriend texted me he's parked at B-15. Do you know where that is?"

"That's right next to where I park. Come on, I'll show you." She walked the girl down a row and then around a corner to where her used Honda Fit awaited.

"There," she said, pointing at a column. "B-15."

Alaska didn't notice two vans stopped nearby. She had no way to know they were positioned exactly to block the views of the only two cameras covering this section.

She did notice when a man opened the side door on one of the vans. She turned to look at him.

There was another noise — behind her. Before she could turn, a hand from behind slapped over her mouth, an arm grabbed her around the waist and Alaska's feet came off the ground.

She saw the other man grab the girl and both of them were rushed to the open van door.

It happened so fast!

Alaska struggled and kicked and belatedly opened her mouth to scream. The man holding her grabbed the inside of her right arm and pinched. The pain was excruciating. Tears sprang to her eyes. She stopped moving — hoping that would stop the pain.

Alaska was tossed into the back of the van on a carpeted floor, then re-grabbed by the same man. He pulled her up against him, holding her with an arm tight on her waist and a hand back over her mouth.

"What the hell?" asked the driver, turning to look at them. Alaska saw only a ball cap pulled low, sunglasses, and a turtleneck sweater pulled up over his chin.

"They were together," said the man holding Alaska. "Can't leave one behind."

"Shit."

The van door closed, blocking out all light except what came from the front. The driver turned back around and the van started moving.

Alaska heard gasping and turned to look at the girl. Her eyes were huge and her chest was moving in and out — fast. She was struggling to breathe. Alaska saw her panic as she wheezed and struggled desperately to get air in her lungs.

The man holding the girl — a sunburned white goon with buzz-cut hair so white it disappeared on his skull — let go of her and shook his head.

"What's wrong with her?"

Alaska grabbed at the fingers covering her mouth. The guy holding her let her speak.

"She's having an asthma attack. Let me help her."

The van jolted to a stop.

"You can help her?" asked the man behind the wheel.

Alaska nodded.

"Help her and I might not have to kill you today."

Alaska stared at him in horror.

"We didn't come for you. Show us you're useful and you might survive. For a time."

Chapter One

Sara Flores
The Downtown Dojo, Tulsa, Oklahoma

I knew this was a bad idea.

My name is Sara Flores and I'm both a private investigator and a werewolf. The werewolf part of me wasn't normally a problem. I guarded that secret like it meant my life — because it probably did.

But today Connor Rockwood was making it a problem.

He had dragged me to this dojo on the eighth floor of a low-rent office building in Tulsa, Oklahoma. The owner is one of his former Special Forces buddies who lets him use the place for workouts when no classes are scheduled.

It was a simple place, with a huge blue mat in the center of the room surrounded by banged-up green lockers for changing, a wall rack of bo fighting sticks, and three orange benches, one of which I was sitting on.

It's my fault I was here. Working with Connor had seemed like a good idea two months ago. That's when I became a private investigator, licensed by the state of Oklahoma. Fifty five hours of classes, pass a test — and voila! — I'm a private eye.

I wanted the license to back off suspicious cops who might find me near dead bodies in parts of town no sane woman would go near. The license gives me an excuse to be there.

And, yes, I've been in the vicinity of a bunch of dead bodies in the two years since I was turned. Finding missing or threatened innocents has become my calling and the assholes who take them aren't interested in giving them up. Not without a fight.

"C'mon, Flores." Connor grabbed my arm and dragged me out on the mat. We were both in street clothes, but barefoot.

"You can't learn Krav Maga up here, darlin'." He pointed to my head. "Your body has to learn it too." He had a slight Tennessee drawl that normally made me smile since it came from a body built like a Sherman tank.

Today I wasn't smiling.

"I'm not paying you to teach me martial arts," I said, surprised at how defensive I sounded. "I have a brown belt. What I want is all the street-fighting strategy you learned in Special Forces."

"That's what I'm tryin' to teach you."

He eyed me, pursing his lips. "Big, bad, brown belt, huh? Show me some moves."

My eyes narrowed. If he smiled, I was going to have to kill him.

This was a very bad idea.

I'd met Connor when I hired him to bodyguard my very first client. She'd been run off the road and had her house bombed by a man determined to kill her. I'd stashed the two of us in a hotel suite and hired Connor to protect her while I was asleep. He'd done a good job — hence my decision to hire him for this.

Connor reached across the two feet between us and pushed my shoulder. Provoking me.

I took the push without moving my feet and imagined him with a big wolf-sized bite out of his shoulder. I was careful not to smile.

He threw up his hands. "This is a bad idea."

Well... at least we agreed on that.

"Just teach me the moves," I said, also throwing up my hands. "What's with you? You want us to spar? You're eight inches taller than me, outweigh me by more than 100 pounds, and you're a man. And former Special Forces. What are you trying to prove?"

"And who do you think you'll be fighting — teenage girls?"

I wanted to scream.

I'd *love* to test myself against Connor — because I didn't know who would win. And I need to know because the next man trying to kill me might have his skills. My life might depend on it. Thanks to my wolf, I've been stronger than any man I've gone up against in the two years since my transformation. But none of them were at Connor's skill level.

The problem is, Connor would know immediately there was something wrong about me. Beaten — or almost beaten — by a woman? He'd never let that go without answers. Thus far only two people know what I am. They're both my friends but it makes my skin crawl that they know.

No way I'm adding Connor to that list.

He snapped his fingers in front of my eyes. "This won't work. You can't teach heart or guts. A person either has them or not and you, little girl, don't have either."

I smiled. He was still trying to provoke me, but I was immune to macho posturing.

He raised his eyebrows. "That's funny? Your next client won't think so when you get her killed because you can't protect her."

I lunged forward and slammed my right fist — twisting it — aiming directly at his throat.

I wasn't even aware I was moving until my fist was almost there and, horrified, I tried to stop.

Connor got his forearm up to block me — he'd been expecting something, after all. My fist hit his forearm and I heard a very faint crack.

We broke apart.

He grabbed his left forearm, his eyes wide in surprise.

I grabbed my right hand. Instead of a soft neck, my knuckles had hit bone and I'd broken at least two of them. The pain was so bad it made my eyes water, but I had to hide it. Tomorrow my knuckles would be healed. No way to explain that except that they were never damaged.

I bent over until the urge to scream in pain stopped.

"I'm sorry," I said. "I moved before I thought. I didn't think you could get to me. What did you say..."

Connor moved the fingers on his damaged arm and winced. He looked back at me, evaluating.

"My fault," he said. "Nothing was working. Saying you'd get a client killed — I went too far. But — hell Flores. That was so fast I barely saw it. And strong."

"You have pain moving some of those fingers, don't you?" I asked.

He stared at me.

"I have really good hearing and I heard a crack. I think your ulna is fractured."

He kept staring at me.

I closed my eyes. Fractures take a long time to heal. Time he wouldn't be able to do his normal bodyguard work.

All my fault.

I walked over to the bench and picked up Connor's cell phone.

"Stick your thumb on here so I can call Judy. She'll get you checked out." I turned away from him to dial, hiding the broken knuckles on my hand.

"Judy? It's Sara. Could you do a job for me? Connor needs the best orthopedic guy in Tulsa. His ulna bone is fractured — hopefully just a hairline."

I handed the phone to Connor and left. I could feel his eyes on my back.

FREE STORY DOWNLOAD

NOT AVAILABLE ANYWHERE ELSE!

Werewolves and Holidays

Sometimes I write poor Sara Flores into a corner and even I can't figure out how she's going to survive. That's when I take a week off and write a short story. Typically about a case involving her and some holiday.

I offer the story exclusively to anyone who joins my monthly author mailing list. (It's not available elsewhere.)

You can get your free story by going to: SueDenver.com. Right on the home page there will be a story for the current holiday and a signup to get it for free. Which holiday? You won't know until you check it out!

ABOUT THE AUTHOR

Did you ever want to be more than yourself? I always have. As a kid, I imagined I lived up in the clouds with a band of other kids. We would swoop down — because we could fly! — and rescue people in trouble. And we'd beat the crap out of their abusers.

When I got older, I became obsessed with crime and mysteries. I wanted to know how someone could track down evil doers and exposing them to the world.

The day I quit my corporate job — my dreams came true. Today I spend my days throwing my character, Sara Flores, at one criminal mastermind after another — just to see what she can do.

And... I cheated. I let her be more than herself by making her a werewolf — the only magical creature in a world otherwise just like ours. Because I wanted to see what she could do with a wolf's senses and strength. And wildness.

So join me for stories of ruthless criminals, suspicious cops, and Sara's small band of misfits fighting to save us all. Test drive my world with a free story at SueDenver.com.

ALSO BY SUE DENVER

Available now from the author or at your favorite booksellers

Shop.SueDenver.com

BOOK 2: SARA FLORES, WEREWOLF P.I. SERIES: Private Investigator Sara Flores was hired to find a woman who left her Tulsa casino job 192 days ago - and hasn't been seen since. The cops say Alaska Brown left willingly. The FBI isn't looking. And now, someone deadly is trying to kill off Sara and her team. Someone with unlimited funds. Has she the right to risk all their lives? But... how can she not? Can Sara and her 3-person team of misfits really take down a billionaire — or is this the case that gets them all killed?

BOOK 3, SARA FLORES, WEREWOLF P.I. SERIES: Sara Flores, werewolf P.I., needs to find a young woman who disappeared seeking evidence her father was murdered 12 years ago — instead of dying drugged and stupid in a Wyoming snowstorm. But to do that, Sara has to confront a man who even U.S. presidents have been afraid to touch. [Novel]

BOOK 1: WOLFLADY SERIES. Abandoned. Nobody to show her the ropes. How will she use her new powers? Nobody believes werewolves exist. Neither did Sara Flores until her Lupiti neighbor turned her. He then had the unmitigated gall to die on her, before telling her anything about what to expect. Sara determines to use her new skills for good. But besides saving innocents, what exactly does that mean? Yes, she can track down bullies and evildoers. But, is it okay to kill them? If so, is it okay to eat them? How about if she's really, really hungry?
[Collection: All 7 WolfLady short stories plus one novella — Curiosity Kills. 214 pgs.]

BOOK 2: WOLFLADY SERIES: Payback is a bitch! 3 werewolf vigilante novellas in one boxed set. Rescuing those in need isn't all Sara Flores likes about her new life as a werewolf. Who knew it would be so much fun terrorizing evil doers? The looks on their faces when they discover they're not invincible — it just warms a girl's heart. Set includes: **Betrayal in Oklahoma**, **Amateur Assassin**, *and* **The Stench of Fear.** [*210 Pgs.*]

Printed in Great Britain
by Amazon

57286075R00086